No Windmills in Basra

Deep Vellum Publishing
3000 Commerce St., Dallas, Texas 75226
deepvellum.org · @deepvellum

Deep Vellum is a 501c3 nonprofit literary arts organization founded in
2013 with the mission to bring the world into conversation through
literature.

Originally published in 2018 as ال طواحين هواء ف ي البصرة
by Dār Suṭūr li-l-nashr wa-l-tawzīʿ.

First Deep Vellum Edition, 2022

Library of Congress Control Number: 2022935381

ISBNS: 978-1-64605-186-1 (TPB) | 978-1-64605-187-8 (Ebook)

"The Hat Stand" was published in *World Literature Today* (Spring 2021).
"The Scarecrow" was published in *Granta* 154 (Winter 2021). "The Night
Girl" was published in Vestal Review No. 58 (Spring 2021).

Cover design by Zoe Norvell

Interior layout and typesetting by Haley Chung

PRINTED IN THE UNITED STATES OF AMERICA

No Windmills in Basra

DIAA JUBAILI

translated from the Arabic by

CHIP ROSSETTI

DEEP VELLUM PUBLISHING
DALLAS, TEXAS

"Ah, but what does all this matter?"

—Emma Bovary

There are no windmills in Basra.
Where do I put all these delusions?
Who am I supposed to fight?

Contents

Translator's Note

The characters in Diaa Jubaili's *No Windmills in Basra* have a confounding habit of turning themselves into something else: a eucalyptus tree, a dung beetle, a lighthouse, a butterfly, even water. The stories read at times like modern folktales or urban legends, presenting the reader with inexplicable, sometimes magical events, even as they foreground the violence and war that have overshadowed Iraqis' daily lives for the past several decades. It's what first drew me to Jubaili's work.

In addition to *No Windmills in Basra*, which was published in 2018, Jubaili (b. 1977 in Basra) has published three other short-story collections and nine novels. His fiction has addressed a broad array of themes relevant to the lives of modern Iraqis, particularly in light of the legacies of imperialism, invasion, and war, as well as the complex religious and racial makeup of Iraq's history. His 2017 novel *al-Mashtur* (*The Cloven Man*), for example, centers on the years of sectarian violence that followed the US-led occupation in 2003, in which the Iraqi protagonist is literally cloven in half along religious lines. Other novels of his, such as *Bughiz al-'Ajib* (*The Amazing Bughiz*) and, more recently, *al-Bitriq al-As-wad* (*The Black Penguin*) have focused on characters drawn from the country's sizable African Iraqi population, a minority group—found primarily in Iraq's south—whose presence today is a reflection of the region's legacies of African slavery.

No Windmills in Basra (in Arabic, *La Tawahina hawa' fi l-Basra*) offers an unusual combination of playfulness and the serious: the stories' whimsy is often undercut by darker realities and glimpses of tragedy. It is also Jubaili's first collection centered on very short stories. With a few exceptions, most of the book's seventy-six stories fall under what is now known in English as "flash fiction," commonly defined as fiction of 1,500 words or less. In contemporary Arabic literature, the "very short story" (*al-qissa al-qasira jiddan*) is perhaps most closely associated with the Syrian author Zakariya Tamer (b.1931), although other authors have also written in it. In an interview I conducted with Jubaili for *The Vestal Review* online magazine, he stated that, in his opinion, this genre "is still in its stage of growth, where [Arabic] readers accustomed to longer texts like the novel and short story are still trying to wrap their heads around it."

Along with the metamorphoses mentioned above, Jubaili's stories include fantastic elements, such as Walt Whitman's beard growing wildly over a public park, a young man who sheds salt, and a woman with sparrows in her ribcage. Perhaps unsurprisingly, critics have compared Jubaili's writings to the tradition of Latin American magical realism. In the same interview, he discusses his introduction to short-form fiction via his readings of

Spanish-language authors such as Eduardo Galeano, Juan José Arreola, Julio Cortázar, and Augusto Monterroso, as well as other well-known practitioners of the form, including Chekhov and O. Henry. But in a 2017 interview with *Jil Jadid* magazine, he said that contemporary magical realism had only an "indirect" influence on him. Instead, he emphasized the importance of magic and fantasy in Arabic folktales as a source for his fiction, including the stories he heard from his own grandmother, which were like "training for the encounter with magical realism." On a broader level, he noted, "There are always lines of juxtaposition between the real and the fantastic . . . What I write is nothing but our Iraqi reality, filled with the strange and the wondrous, the magical and the irrational."

Indeed, the city of Basra—where he still lives—is the setting for almost all these stories and plays a key role in his fiction. The largest city in Iraq's south, Basra lies on the vital Shatt al-'Arab waterway that flows out into the Gulf and is famous for its palm trees. Crucially, the Shatt al-'Arab also forms the border with Iran to the east, and during the prolonged Iran-Iraq War (1980–88), Basra and its environs were on the front line of fighting and consequently suffered heavily from bombardment. Jubaili was four when the war broke out, and in interviews he has spoken about the indelible impressions that scenes of war and bloodshed make on a child's mind.

At the same time, the stories in *No Windmills in Basra* are filled with wordplay and puns, which give the stories a light-hearted playfulness even when dealing with more serious issues. Wordplay is notoriously difficult to translate, particularly when it plays the central role it does in many of these stories. In some instances, I was able to take advantage of a fortuitous overlap between Arabic and English, but other stories required translational workarounds, which I hope capture at least some of the resonances of the original.

A few stories here rely for their effect on a cultural familiarity that most English-language readers will not have, and in those cases, I have added a brief note in brackets at the end of the stories. I hope these relatively rare intrusions of explanatory material do not interfere with the enjoyment of the book, particularly for those readers who don't need them.

Chip Rossetti
Cranford, New Jersey
June 2021

Wars

Flying

Mubarak, who worked as a security guard for thousands of chickens at a poultry plant south of Basra, had never dreamed of flying. But he flew twice—not on a plane, or by means of a hot-air balloon or a parachute, and not even on a giant demon's wings or a magic carpet, as happens so often in tales from the *Thousand and One Nights*. Nor was he an admirer of the medieval scientist-inventor Ibn Firnas, who dreamed of flapping wings and soaring heights, since Mubarak knew that with that sort of thing, he would eventually end up a pile of broken bones on the side of the road.

Simply put, Mubarak flew in a way he hadn't planned previously, in an acrobatic, dramatic, mad fashion that only happens to people in their imagination, or when they're losing their mind.

The first time Mubarak flew was during the withdrawal of the Iraqi army at the end of the 1991 Gulf War. He flew for a few seconds the moment a bomb hit an IFA W50 truck carrying more than forty soldiers, including him, as they fled from American air bombardments.

All the soldiers were blown to pieces, their limbs flying in all directions. Except for him. Miraculously, he survived. His collarbone and shoulder were broken from the impact of hitting the sandy ground in Safwan. Although he was airborne for only a matter of seconds, Mubarak was inclined to joke and laugh about it as much as he could. Once he'd regained consciousness and recovered from the airstrike, he started telling his friends and relatives about the trip he'd taken. His miraculous flight over the desert sands.

"I met a lot of birds, and I maneuvered a Patriot missile that was on its way to intercept an Iraqi surface-to-surface missile. And from way up there, I even spotted General Schwarzkopf. He and the Iraqi Minister of Defense were signing the surrender agreement!"

That's what Mubarak would say, and everyone who heard him would laugh. One of them would slap him on the shoulder, forgetting that was where he had been injured, and there would be some more loud laughs, more jokes about the "flying soldier," more levity, and more guffaws.

When the third war broke out in 2003, Mubarak was nearly fifty. His head and shoulder had begun leaning to the left when he walked. Because of his injury, he had grown a hump on his back, and consequently he was entitled to a government pension. But it was a very small pension, not enough to support his family of eleven. So he was forced to take a job as a security guard at a poultry plant not far from where he lived. He spent most of his time there. The annoying clucking of the chickens deafened his ears, and the stench of excrement filled his nose. He was at risk of bird flu, which from time to time had an outbreak among the chickens. But Mubarak didn't care about all that: he had lived through some tough situations, not the least of which was his near-death flight, which had become a local legend that people joked about.

On several occasions, he had escaped getting killed in war, and dodged bullets and bombs by the skin of his teeth, so why should he worry about a disease carried by weak and foolish creatures like chickens?

"I will die like a high-flying bird!" Mubarak repeated to himself—but as a joke, not seriously. Although someone had once predicted that fate for him—a Gypsy woman who read his future to his mother when he was little.

During one of that war's haphazard airstrikes, an American plane bombed the poultry plant, making mincemeat out of all the chickens. Since he seemed to be required to fly in every war, people living in the area began to wonder whether Mubarak had flown this time, too. They hurried over to the plant, but found nothing but the destruction that had befallen it. Their hearts were filled with despair, a despair at the prospect of stumbling on his corpse, which seemed to have been crushed along with the unfortunate chickens.

But all of a sudden, while they were shouting for him, they saw him emerge from beneath the rubble. He was smeared with blood and covered in feathers from head to toe.

He was staggering left and right, flapping his arms like wings.

He was flying.

Flying.

The Saltworks

At first the doctors thought that he had psoriasis. That was before his grandmother discovered, by chance, what was coming off of him whenever he scratched somewhere on his body. It was salt.

"It's salt!" she cried, as she tasted a bit of the white scab that flew into the air while she was examining his hair. Then she summoned everyone in the family to taste those tiny bits for themselves.

"You see?" she asked, amid the family's stunned faces. "Didn't I tell you he was salty?!"

Everyone in his immediate family, as well as several relatives, stood around him. They began moistening their fingers with saliva, wiping them on his arm and his face, and then licking them. They stared at each other in amazement. As if the taste of it delighted them, they did it again just to be certain that what they had just tried out was real or whether their imagination was playing tricks on them. His older sister didn't believe it, it made her sick to her stomach, and she blamed the whole thing on a group delusion affecting their sense of taste. One of the aunts criticized her, saying in a scolding tone, "If there's any delusion here, it's in your head, young lady. All this salt and you're calling it a delusion?"

Year after year, Jamal continued on his way to becoming a salty creature. That didn't bother his family. His mother didn't even buy salt anymore, since he provided all the good salt she needed for cooking. Anything extra that she didn't need she gave to the neighbors.

Other than this unusual condition, Jamal didn't suffer from any health problem. In fact, just the opposite: the more salt his body produced, the more immune he grew to illnesses, especially in the summer. That's when his pores secreted great quantities of sweat, which soon turned into layers of salt that collected on the surface of his skin. His mother began scraping it off as soon as he woke up in the morning, collecting about a kilogram of salt free of impurities. This phenomenon no longer caused him concern. He had gotten used to his unusual situation since childhood, and he was accustomed to having people call him "Salty Jamal" or "Saltman." He wasn't the object of envy: no one wanted a son that produced such an enormous amount of salt. His aunts on his father's side wished he knew how to replace the salt with gold dust, but his aunts on his mother's side would have preferred it were diamonds.

"But . . . salt?" one of them asked, in a tone of despair. "What could be cheaper than salt?"

"Dirt!" replied another.

"Now all we need is a boy that sheds dust so we can all get asthma!"

The boys at school began to tease him. They bullied him any chance they could.

"You just need a few spices, and then we can put you in the oven!"

He wasn't one to take their bullying sitting down, so he took some of his salt and threw it in their eyes. His responses always silenced them:

"At least salt is better than the lice you've got living in your hair and armpits!"

Life was good for his family in those days, until war broke out in 1980. Jamal was conscripted and vanished in the grind of war, in a cursed spot in the Basra region that the soldiers came to know as "the Saltworks." It was located west of the city of Faw, the southernmost point in Iraq, where the bloodiest battles took place.

Some survivors of the war said that he was killed, but they never found his body. Others said he was taken prisoner by the Iranians, but that only little bits of news about him—a letter or a telegram—reached his family. The war ended, and everyone got tired of waiting. As the years went by, there were rumors that all traces of Jamal were lost, until his name eventually became short-hand for "loss," "disappearance," and "vanishing forever."

Only his mother, whose life and cooking had lost all their flavor, spent the rest of her days repeatedly going to the Red Cross headquarters in Basra to ask what had become of her son, whose remains had never been found in that salty area, as though he had come from salt and to salt he returned. She would stay all day there, asking everyone who came and went about Jamal and holding his picture up to passersby, as she repeated the phrase she became known for:

"My son Jamal! He was a lump of salt and he dissolved!"

The Gross-Out Olympics

Khadduri burped a lot. He had been unable to control it, ever since he was a kid, sucking his thumb and putting his toes in his mouth. He would let out belches that gas-relief tonics or sugar-water couldn't help with. As soon as he tasted something, even if it was just water, he began burping. He'd let loose a burst of air from his stomach and out of his mouth with a noise that was more like a bull's snort. It was something that frequently caused him embarrassment.

Khadduri had gotten into the habit of letting people know whatever it was he'd been tasting or eating each time he burped. When he ate chicken, he burped and then said "Chicken." When he ate fish, he burped and said "Seafood!" It was the same with all the other foods, or matters in life and situations that came his way.

It might happen that Khadduri would give a different impression about what he was tasting or what was happening to him—expressing either his disgust or his delight in it. When he disappeared one day, and then suddenly showed up again looking like a mess, they asked him where he had been. He let out a long, bitter burp, and said, "Shit!" And they knew at once that he had been in jail.

When he burped and said, "Ruin!" they knew he had gotten married.

When he burped and said, "Soot!" they knew he had been drafted for the war. There, in the barracks near the border where he ended up, he heard that some of the soldiers were organizing a secret Gross-Out Olympics.

In addition to a Burping Contest, there were other competitions, such as Fastest Masturbation, Loudest Fart, Farthest Urination, and Spitting. Most of the soldiers participated in the masturbation competition, eager to look through the nudie magazines that were specially brought in to turn on the participants.

Three soldiers were competing with Khadduri in the burping contest. The first one had started things off with a powerful burp and then let them know what he'd been eating, saying, "Leeks!" The second soldier burped and said, "Beans!" Then the third soldier burped and said, "Combat boots!" Khadduri hadn't put anything in his stomach, but when it was his turn to burp, something unprecedented happened: with no warning, a bomb landed in the middle of the soldiers in the parade ground. Thick smoke spread everywhere, and not a sound could be heard from any of them. There was no groaning from the injured, only the sound of Khadduri's footsteps, as he got up among the mangled bodies and staggered, unsteady on his feet. Smoke rose up from his torn body, until he fell to his knees and burped for the last time, bitterly crying out, "Deeeaaaaaaath!"

Nation

In addition to his hands, Wasam lost his entire extended family to a Cruise missile launched from an American aircraft carrier during the Gulf War in 1991. It landed on their house in Basra. He was six months old then, and the photo of him as he was, injured and without hands, kept showing up in newspapers and on television news channels, until an Australian family decided to adopt him.

And so, Wasam was brought via the Red Cross to Melbourne, and within a month's time, he was a member of that family. He thrived in their embrace. They called him Mark and lavished all kinds of care and affection on him. At age five, he learned to write with his right foot, and over time he got to be very good at it, so much so that he had no problem doing his classwork once he started school. Then he began using a computer, and eventually mastered the art of drawing with both feet. He was a clever boy of many talents. His disability didn't keep him from his favorite hobbies, like football, drawing, reading, and writing, since he had gotten used to tapping the computer keyboard with his toes in order to write his stories and personal essays. All that time, his role model was the Irish writer Christy Brown: he had read his novel, *My Left Foot*, and was impressed by it, when his adoptive father gave it to him as a present for his tenth birthday. Afterward, he saw the film about Brown's life story, and ever since that day, he had hoped to write his own story, too. He was obsessed with Daniel Day Lewis, who played the role of Christy Brown to perfection. At the same time, he could see his adoptive mother in Bridget Brown, the mother, who was played by Brenda Fricker.

Wasam turned thirteen, having believed, over all those past years, that he was Australian, and that he had lost his hands in a car accident, as he had been told. It was something that kept his adoptive family up at night, and as a result, they decided to tell him the truth before he learned it himself by seeing a news report about him from thirteen years before, or maybe by eventually coming across someone—like a friend from school—who would tell him about it.

It happened precisely one night before the American attack on Baghdad in 2003, in the presence of a psychiatrist. His mother had taken it upon herself to tell him, while the other members of his Australian family stood around him and waited for his reaction, to see how he would deal with a piece of news like that. Ideas raced through their minds—one of them expected he would break out into tears, while another one anticipated he would collapse to the floor, and a third imagined he would be angry and blame his parents for waiting so long to tell him the truth that he was adopted.

But none of that happened. It was as if he already knew about everything his mother was struggling with, as she tried to break the news to him gently and soften the blow that he might face. The boy seemed calm, and he gave no indication that betrayed a sense of confusion or bitter consternation, or even a feeling of disappointment. He looked around him, and fixed his gaze on their faces, as if to say, "Pay no mind: this woman who is sitting beside me is my mother, and this man sitting to my right is my father, and that's my grumpy sister, and that boy sitting next to her is my brother, and this house is my house, and Australia is my country." But he didn't say any of that. He didn't utter a single word. Even so, everyone felt the tension go out of the room. Wasam had seemingly survived the ordeal. As they knew, he was a clever, level-headed boy, never one to lose his cool, and here he was now, swallowing the bitter truth like a good sport.

Afterward, the doctor pulled out a map of the world and placed it in front of Wasam on the living room table. Then he asked him to point out where Iraq was on the map, forgetting that the boy had no hands to point at things. While the doctor was trying to make light of the reaction everyone had to his obvious gaffe, Wasam bent over the map to mark the spot where Iraq was with his lips.

His kiss made a sound much like the sound of someone putting his lips around his mother's nipple for the first time.

The Scarecrow

Just at the time of the ceasefire between Iraq and Iran in 1988, an infantry platoon discovered that they were in a minefield. They found that out from Private First Class Hakim, who had stepped on a mine.

They were terrified, but they didn't leave him on his own, at least for the first half of that day. After that, one by one, they started to withdraw, ostensibly to go get help, but each time one of them left, he never came back.

Private First Class Hakim stayed there all alone. He didn't budge an inch, for fear of setting off the mine and—at a minimum—losing his leg. That is, if the mine didn't turn him into a pile of body parts.

As time passed, once word had gotten out that the war was officially over, the area where he found himself planted was marked off with barbed wire and warning signs indicating it was a minefield. Farmers returned to their fields and restored them, planting different kinds of crops until they turned green and ripened. After all that, among the scarecrows in the neighboring fields, Private First Class Hakim became known as the Minefield Scarecrow.

Those other scarecrows saw him shooing away crows and eagles, to keep them from carrying off the bones of the platoon members that had lain scattered in the field for years, those who had left but none of whom ever came back.

The Taste of Death

When Atwan returned to his hometown on the Faw Peninsula southeast of Basra, two years after the Iran-Iraq War, he found his land had turned into a brackish salt bog.

Salt covered every inch of that plot of land. There was no trace of the palm trees whose leaves once shaded great expanses of fields cultivated with henna. Grief came over him when he cast his eyes over his ruined land. He remembered his childhood, his adolescence, and his young manhood in this patch of land where he grew up and spent the best years of his life, before it was transformed into the site of vicious, savage battles over the course of the war. Tens of thousands of Iraqi and Iranian soldiers had fallen there, and it was still an operating zone for the Red Cross, whose workers were digging up ground to search for the remains of missing soldiers from both sides. But there was one thing that always hindered their work: the mines that the government had so far been unable to clear. And now the soil had turned fallow, desolate, and lifeless.

Suddenly, as if someone had put the idea into his head, Atwan decided he would bring the soil back to life.

* * *

Only a few days later, Atwan took up his task with the help of his five sons. They all worked with enthusiasm and energy. They removed the salt from the ground's surface, then began purifying, tilling, and fertilizing the soil. Then they scattered seed and set up scarecrows stuffed with straw, dressing them in dead people's clothes—clothes that ordinarily would have been dumped into dry riverbeds. They stood there and pictured the plot of land blooming with specific kinds of vegetables—tomatoes, cucumbers, potatoes, spinach, beans, and chard. All that left was the watering phase. For that, Atwan considered bringing in fresh water via big tanker trucks. It would be expensive, but not impossible. But this Basra peasant, who was approaching sixty, was too stubborn to be easily thwarted. And so, the next day, fifteen tanker trucks filled with fresh water made their way to the patch of land, and they all proceeded to water it, until it was irrigated, flooded, and nearly choked with water.

After it was all done, Atwan stood on his land with his hands on his hips, casting his eye over what he had accomplished. He imagined the land transformed into a verdant orchard as it had been in the past, filled with fruits, vegetables, and other crops. His face broke into a smile and hope returned to him. He felt satisfaction: his dreams were coming true, and it would be only a few months before he could reap the fruits of his labor.

But something unexpected happened, something he hadn't counted on.

One day, at sunset, following a day of irrigating with fresh water, a platoon of soldiers that had been buried beneath the earth since the war rose up and started walking away. The Basra peasant was startled and could feel guilt gnawing at his heart, as if he had kicked them out of his own house, rather than from his land. He put his hands to his head and groaned, to the surprise and puzzlement of his sons. He ran after the soldiers until he caught up with them. There were fourteen of them, all weighted down with the mud that had accumulated over time. He didn't know who they were, but that wasn't his concern. He brought them to a halt and pleaded with them to return to his land.

"I beg your pardon, soldiers," he told them. "I didn't mean to disturb you. If I had known you were resting in this plot of land, I would never have dared wake you!"

"Don't bother, sir," one of them replied, as he re-inserted his right eyeball, which had suddenly slid out of its socket. "From now on, there's no place for us in this soil."

"Why?" he asked pleadingly. "Where do you want to go?"

"Somewhere else," another soldier answered, plucking a rusty bullet out of his head. "A place that has a sufficient supply of salt."

"Salt?!" he shouted, thunderstruck. "Why do you need salt?"

His five sons overheard this remarkable conversation between their father, the agitated Basran peasant, and a platoon of dead soldiers. They stood there, mouths agape in astonishment.

"Are you stupid, sir, or just ignorant?" one of the soldiers asked. He spat out a fragment that had lodged in his throat.

"I'll tell you why we're leaving your land," said another soldier, shoving his stiff intestines back through the gash a bomb had made in his stomach. "After you leached the salt out of the topsoil, with all that massive amount of fresh water that you poured over our bones, we felt our deaths had lost their taste."

"That's right, sir!"

One of the fourteen soldiers, fumbling with his Adam's apple so it wouldn't fall out of his throat, chimed in hoarsely, "It's because of you our death will never have a taste again!"

Then they left.

Inheritance

I can imagine how sad and shocking it is when a woman doesn't reply to her son's letters when he's a prisoner of war. But at any rate I knew that my mother didn't know how to read or write. So I wasn't sad or shocked. Although she could have asked someone else for help—a neighbor, a relative, a stranger, or even one of the passersby that hurried past our house every day as she sat by the front door, waiting for me there in the hopes that I might return. He could have read her my letter, and once he finished, she could have dictated her response to him, and he could have written it down on a piece of paper that she then could have placed in the box at the Red Cross, so it could find its way to me.

But she didn't do that. I wasn't sad or shocked about that, either.

The years passed, slow and oppressive. During those years I would write to her periodically—a letter every month—enclosing words expressing my love for her and my desire to return and embrace her again after such a long absence. I kept doing that for a long time, even though in the end I knew I would never get an answer from her. That meant either she was dead, or she hadn't found anyone who could write back for her. Mostly I thought she was dead. I was her only son, and I was afraid to write anything to other relatives, fearing that one of them would send me the agonizing news that my mother had died. Back then, news of her death would have made me very sad, much more than if it had happened while I was with her in her final days. At least that would have comforted her soul.

After thirteen years, we were released from prison and returned home to Iraq. The road there was long and tedious. Some of us started singing softly, and others were fast asleep. And there were some who distracted themselves by staring at the scenery of mountains and fields along the road. I wished I could kill time by reading, the way I used to do before I was taken prisoner, when I was on long trips. But for lack of a book to amuse myself with, I occupied my time thinking about how things would be after I got back. Suddenly, I found myself imagining my mother's face when she saw me for the first time after all those years. She would examine me, searching for any trace of bullets on my chest. She would have gotten old now, and the waiting would have deepened the wrinkles on her face. For a moment, I imagined I could catch the scent of her—the smell of musk that she always wore as a perfume, and that lingered with me whenever she embraced me before I went out. I remembered the last time, when I left the house to join my military unit. I will never forget her warm hands on my chest as she muttered prayers and verses from the Qur'an.

When I got to the house, I couldn't find my mother. I was told that she had died—not years before, as I had assumed, but only a few months ago. All she had left behind was a bundle of my letters in the closet. I hurried over to it and started going through her clothes and shawls—their scent distracted me, and I sat down to smell them while I sobbed like a lost, orphaned child. Afterward, I resumed my search for those letters until I found them. They were wrapped in a piece of green cloth, just like you would wrap the Qur'an. As soon as I opened it, the scent of apples wafted up from it, and I pictured the many times my mother had rubbed the ˙cloth on the golden grillwork of saints' tombs. I took the letters out of their envelopes, one after the other. I could grieve this time and feel shock.

My mother had never understood the letters.

It wasn't just because she couldn't read or write. But it was my bad habit of crying whenever I wrote her a letter. Or rather, it was that superior ability my tears possessed to distort words, to enlarge and jostle them, and so turn them into traces of gushing tears, stains devoid of meaning.

Graveyard

Nasir was leaving behind him a trail that showed where he'd been.

He was naked and torn when the dead found him sprawled on a large gravestone in the cemetery of the world. Ever since then, as soon as he passed by a place or sat down there, you could see the dirt he left behind him, a damp, reddish, sorrowful dirt that made death loathsome to those who are already dead.

It was a strange phenomenon that had never occurred before in the world of the dead, who bring nothing but burial-shrouds with them from the world of the living. All except Nasir, who was still scattering dirt on places that lay beyond nonexistence. The only thing the dead could do about it was ask him what kind of work he had done in the world of the living and where he got all that dirt from.

That's when he told them, with a bitter expression that he nearly choked on:

"I was a soldier and this is the nation's soil!"

The Frog

Alwan was accustomed to sticking his nose where it didn't belong.

While he was looking for what he wanted in a display case at the supermarket, by chance he saw some strange pieces of frozen meat, carefully wrapped and hidden beneath the pile of chicken thighs. Later, he realized it was frog meat.

Alwan registered a complaint with the health inspector's office. And indeed, the health inspection team found great quantities of it. But he was surprised they didn't confiscate that disgusting variety of meat. When he asked why, he was told that it was legal and displayed for sale—along with octopus, small shark, and turtle meat—for Chinese and Filipino workers in the oil fields near the border. However, the owner of the supermarket had to pay a fine for poor storage.

On his way back home, Alwan saw some boys playing with frogs, throwing them at each other. Just then, an idea popped into his head.

"I'll sell fresh frogs," he said, jubilantly snapping his fingers. "It's got to be a profitable business."

The next day, he brought a fishhook and a bunch of worms to a neglected, brackish river, a tributary of the Shatt al-'Arab, where there were plenty of frogs. He hunted a lot of them. He began cutting them up and wrapping them, with the help of his wife, who went along with this business project of his, since he'd promised her some respectable profits. The profits surpassed expectations once he sold the first batch of frogs to the Chinese and Filipinos working in the Majnun Nafti oil field.

Alwan continued with this profitable line of work until a day came when he caught only a single frog. Nevertheless, he cast his fishing tackle into the still waters of the river, in the hope of catching another one. Luck was with him this time, when he caught a giant frogman who had been hiding there beneath the algae ever since the Iran-Iraq War.

"Who are you? Iraqi or Iranian?" the frogman asked, wheeling around in all directions. He shaded his eyes with his algae- and wart-covered hand, to shield them from the burning midday sun.

"Is the war over?"

Love

The Scent of His Shirt

He used to dream of her abaya, and when she gave it to him, he wanted to give her something as a memento in return. She asked him for his shirt.

"I wouldn't dream of asking anything more than that. And it smells like you!"

So he took it off and handed it to her.

"This shirt is like a dream. Hide it well," he told her with a wink. A smile played on his lips before he added, "It might fly away!"

That night, she sat down and thought about what he had said. It seemed like he was joking, or so she thought at first—after all, what would make shirts fly away? Even so, as though she were taking what he said seriously, she bit her lower lip and said:

"The wind!"

Yes, the wind carried off everything. She considered using clothespins to fix the shirt in place on the washline, if she thought about washing it the next day. That way the wind couldn't make it fly away. But in any case, she wasn't going to wash it, so it could keep the smell of him.

It was no simple matter for a woman to keep her lover's shirt at her house, so she started looking for a safe place to hide it. She wouldn't dream of the closet, of course, or the clothes rack, or of keeping it in boxes, wardrobes or dresser drawers. By the same token, she wouldn't think of wearing it, since that would attract the attention of other people in the house, especially in summertime, when she wouldn't be able to wear overcoats and blouses that could keep it out of sight.

Suddenly, an idea popped into her head. To hide it well and hold on to it, and avoid the risk of having it fly away, while keeping the scent of it nearby, she slipped the pillowcase off her pillow and put the shirt over it. Then she put the pillowcase back on over it. Only something happened—something that remained hidden to her all night long. But she paid no attention to it, and she fell asleep with the smell of the shirt in her nose.

When she woke up the next morning, there was nothing under her head except the pillowcase.

"The shirt flew away!" she cried. She realized her mistake: she should have known that the pillow was stuffed with feathers.

Smiles

What Layla loved most about his face were those dimples, curved like a bow, that time had etched over the years, until they seemed more like two grooves on the sides of his mouth, especially when he smiled at her.

She would do anything to make his radiant, bow-like smile appear. She would deliberately make him laugh, tickle him, or tell him jokes. Or, at the very least, she would smile at him, since she knew that what most made him happy was seeing her smile. Layla learned his smile by heart the way someone in love learns a love poem by heart. She would trace her fingers over it, and since she was also a poet, she would write poems about it. It was always the first thing she recollected the moment she woke up.

But Qays, a shepherd and crafter of chaste love poems, spun his own fate at the end of the story. For he knew that Layla would never be his. So he decided to disappear, and leave her to live her life. But he wouldn't do it without finding some way for her to remember him forever. He thought about a lot of things, but in the end, he could think of nothing that his Layla loved more than his smile. At once, an idea occurred to him, and he set off to carry it out that same day.

*   *   *

Quite a long time passed, while Layla looked for Qays, who had vanished without a trace near the place by a river where she used to meet with him every time she went to do her washing. He would play a certain tune on his ney—the only one he knew—and she would ignore her female companions and head to a nearby pond surrounded by a thicket. She would find him waiting for her, sitting on a rock and flashing her his curved smile. They would talk together for a while, they would laugh, and they would hold hands. But soon a feeling of despair would descend on them, after they repeated the same conversation each time:

"Come with me."

"I can't. They will catch up with us!"

"I'll protect you."

"You won't be able to!"

But Qays didn't turn up that afternoon. Likewise, there was no trace of his sheep. Without him, the place seemed desolate, silent, and strange, as if life was absent there. Even the pond had dried up, and the reeds around it were withering away.

Layla went back to her companions on the river bank. But over the following months she kept going back to visit the place where the two of them had once met. Every time she left and headed home, the scent of him didn't linger on her hands, as it had in days past. When despair didn't come over her too quickly, she attempted to trace his footsteps. She would ask strangers, madmen, messengers, herdsmen, knights, storytellers, and poets about him. But none of them had seen him anywhere or heard anything about him. The last person she turned to was a wandering woman fortuneteller, who asked her, "Is he a poet?"

"Yes—that's him!" Layla answered.

The fortuneteller read her tea leaves, and said, in a tone of ill omen, "I see here a poet looking for . . . "

"For what?"

"For a desert!"

"A desert?" Layla asked anxiously. "What is a poet doing in a desert?"

"He is there to die."

Layla didn't believe that fortuneteller. But she resolved to forget about Qays and her past life. And she almost succeeded, if something hadn't happened that at last brought back to her the memory of her lover.

One spring day, when the sun was shining and warm, Layla went out as usual accompanied by some other women, to clean her husband's clothes on the river bank. With the action of the laundry detergent, a thick foam spread over the surface of the water. Some fish stuck their mouths out of the water and blew large rainbow-colored bubbles that rose up, carrying smiles within them.

They were the smiles of those who had drowned.

Even though there were so many of them, Layla recognized the smile of her beloved. It was squeezed between two bow-shaped curves.

[Note: This story references the romantic legend of the poet Qays ibn al-Mulaw-wah, known as "Majnun Layla" ("Layla's Madman"). Qays was a shepherd who went mad after his beloved Layla married another man. Having lost his reason, he ended up living among wild animals in the wilderness. Majnun and Layla's tragic story became the subject of numerous romances and paintings, and he is the supposed author of a number of early Arabic poems about his thwarted love. See also the story "A Hundred Laylas and One Wolf" below.]

Messages

Mishtaq spent his evenings on the riverbank, lingering there until late at night, sipping from a bottle of local wine and singing or weeping over being apart from his beloved Shamma, who had been forced to marry someone else whose house was on the other side of the river. It just so happened that one night, Mishtaq lit a match and brought it up to the cigarette trembling between his lips. He noticed a light on the opposite bank that flashed for a few seconds before disappearing. The match had burned down, singeing his thumb and forefinger, so he lit another one in order to see that other light again as it flickered and then disappeared a few moments later.

Mishtaq had no doubt that the source of that light was his stolen beloved, Shamma. She had recognized the light of his cigarettes, having experienced over the years the blazing flames of his love for her, and so she'd started playing an amusing lovers' game with him. Whenever he lit a match, she responded by doing the same, and they continued like that for more than a year, during which Mishtaq used up thousands of boxes of matches.

He got tired of it, though, and decided to replace the matches with a lighter.

After another year had passed, he hit upon a new method: a flashlight.

Mishtaq still emitted his obsessive beam of light every night. Neither summer heat nor winter cold nor autumn storms kept him from carrying out his beloved ritual, until one day, when he was about to leave the river bank, he sensed that he was now unable to move. Once the sun rose, a boat with a man and a woman on board passed in front of him. The woman was scanning for something along the river's edge, but it didn't seem like she would find it. Meanwhile, the man glared angrily at him.

He wanted to call out to the woman to tell her, "Hey, Shamma! I'm over here! Can't you see me?"

But he couldn't.

He couldn't budge. It was unheard of that a lighthouse like him could ever move an inch, except when it was being torn down.

Salma's Sparrows

Whenever a suitor came forward for Salma, and her family was on the point of approving their marriage, she felt a pain in her chest like a knife.

The pains were intense, like sharp beaks tearing at her from the inside and turning her into a cadaver that was gaunt, worn-out, and perennially stretched thin. It wasn't pleasant for her suitors, who had every hope of marrying a strong, powerful, woman capable of working like a machine, who could be like a busy hatchery and give birth to a dozen children. Not a sick, complaining, useless woman like Salma. Which is what led them to drop their plans to marry her.

After some time, it became clear that what was causing the pains that Salma suffered when a suitor came forward was a group of sparrows in her rib cage. Or, to be precise, that was what the ultrasound at the doctor's office revealed.

"Sparrows?" her mother asked, slapping herself on the cheeks. Her father stood there speechless, hardly believing what he'd heard.

The medical diagnosis hadn't determined exactly how the sparrows had made their way into Salma's chest. Her family turned to quacks who claimed magic cures, and who came to her room in droves. "I have the cure," each one claimed. But in the end, nothing came of them; in fact, just the opposite happened: poor Salma's pain grew worse.

One of those charlatans admitted, "We can sow division between a husband and wife, we can steal someone's willpower, we can summon spirits, we can call on demons, and we can expel jinn from people's bodies. But to drive sparrows out of a girl's ribcage—that's something only poets can do!"

On hearing that, there wasn't a single poet in the city that Salma's family didn't turn to, in the hope of finding some treatment. But none of them got anywhere. The one who was most experienced in the world of poetry told them:

"We write poetry, we can seduce people, we can drift through ethereal realms, but in the end, we're just looking for a desert we can die in. But soothing the fears of sparrows in a woman's breast? That's something only *love* can do!"

"Let the girl fall in love," he added gently. "Don't frighten the sparrows in her heart!"

The Dung Beetle

"There is no more dreadful punishment than futile and hopeless labor."
—Albert Camus

One evening in March, Burhan was returning home on foot. He was miserable and frustrated, having experienced his latest romantic calamity at a woman's hands. She was a student in the university, studying biology—specifically, insect anatomy—and she thought of him as beneath her. He had been trying to win her affection ever since he first saw her in the lab several weeks before, but she broke his heart that morning by turning him down.

Departing from habit, Burhan stuck his hands in his pants pockets, the way spurned lovers do in movies and love stories. He began whistling a sad tune, while kicking the first pebble he happened upon in the street. It was a normal gray pebble, but didn't seem like other pebbles. It was round, as if someone had made it that way, so it would be easy to kick, and would roll freely as far as possible. He continued to kick it all the way home. Burhan noticed—and he didn't know if he was imagining this or if it really was happening—that the pebble was growing a little bigger. He sensed it when he was halfway home, when it seemed heavier than it had originally been. Sometimes he tried to kick it hard, like he would with a ball. It would roll far off and he would forget about it, only to have it appear in front of him again, bigger than it was before.

Burhan didn't go inside his house that day. He preferred to finish this game until the end, and he continued to kick the strange pebble, which had now become the size of a bowling ball, as he played around with it in the city's back streets. He found it an amusing companion, gentler than the unyielding stones lodged in the chests of certain human beings, like that woman studying entomology. Other times he was annoyed with it, and he thought about abandoning it and heading back home, but each time he was about to do that, his curiosity would get the better of him, as he wanted to find out how big it could get. It had reached the size of a football by the time he came upon some bratty kids in the street. They were sitting on the sidewalk, picking their noses and whispering among themselves. Just then, he hit upon the idea of passing it to one of them, and the boy began inviting the others to play football. At least that way they could occupy their free time with something fun instead of sitting in the middle of the road gossiping about girls at their school. Also, Burhan found it a good excuse to be done with this game and go back home. He was already very late, and it had become unreasonable to continue rolling a weird pebble like this all day long. But before that he wanted to get some fun out of it by playing with these boys. So, seized by his old love of football, he joined them. As a kid, he didn't have what it takes to be a skilled player, and he spent plenty of miserable, frustrating time on the reserve bench during games with local teams. But here he was now, drawing on the tricks he still had left in him—lightly and skillfully dribbling the ball, scoring shots into a goal made of two stones, amid the whistling, clapping, and encouragement of these street kids. Less than an hour into it, though, they were starting to get bored and complain about how heavy the pebble was. It hurt their feet when they kicked it, now that it had grown heavier as they played. It had now reached the size of a basketball.

So Burhan found himself alone again with his pebble, which he was forced to roll with the inner side of his foot, so he could keep it moving, taking it from one street to the next. When evening came, that pebble had grown more than he'd expected, such that he was forced to push it with his foot with effort. That slowed his progress, and eventually it wasn't like pushing a ball of wood or cork or cloth. It was a big stone that had nearly turned into a boulder. It was at that point that Burhan decided to quit. He was exhausted, and he felt hungry, thirsty, and worn down. But this time, too, he didn't seem serious about letting it go, without first discovering the mystery of what had been going on since that morning.

He sat on the pebble and started thinking about his past life. He discovered that the work he had done all his life was no less heavy and oppressive and miserable than what he was doing now, as he pushed a pebble that grew as he rolled it. He felt sleepy, so he rested his body against the pebble by the side of the road, laid his head on his arms, and fell asleep. He dreamed that he saw himself above the same pebble, but it was giant size. It was the size of a massive orb, and he started rolling it with his feet like an acrobat, until it had reached the size of our enormous globe. From his vantage point above, he began to observe humans as they destroyed it. From afar, he saw flames blazing up here and there. There were red spots where smoke was rising. He pointed to one of those spots and cried out, "That's where I live!"

He woke up the next morning to the noise of the street cleaners, and the first thing he did was examine the pebble, as he would a car tire, before continuing his advance toward the unknown. He guessed that he wouldn't be able to keep going unless he had something to eat. So he began rolling the pebble toward the market in the city center, where he could have his lunch in a lower-class restaurant. It took him hours to get to the market, and by that time, it was just past noon.

After days and months and years rolling the pebble, moving it from place to place across many streets and neighborhoods, and over bridges, Burhan ended up in the desert. On this journey of his, he had come across plenty of people and strange creatures. He had faced numerous dangers and difficult situations. He had lived through the most awful circumstances—cold, rain, heat, ailments. The blazing sun and icy frost weathered his face, until he came to resemble a disfigured monster. He was ambushed by the fiercest highway robbers, who saw him as just another madman. He ate and drank what people were kind enough to give him, which was enough to provide him with the strength he needed to push the pebble, which was now half his height. It was now a giant ball covered in feces and had a foul, disgusting smell, because he had passed through a sheepherding district where a wretched dog was leading a flock of sheep. The ground covered with the droppings of those timid sheep helped grow the pebble's size and weight. When he left that foul-smelling spot for the desert, Burhan discovered that he was now no longer by himself, for there were thousands of dung beetles engaged in rolling balls of dung with their feet, while he was pushing his ball with his hands. He didn't know if those dung beetles had grown to enormous proportions until they were his size, or if he was the one who had shrunk to their level. It bothered him, but at the same time, he couldn't deny his sense of camaraderie with this group, which continued until he reached a mountain near the border.

Burhan found it strange to come upon a mountain in his path near a city like Basra. But then he recalled that there was a solitary mountain that sat by itself and was called Sanam. One of the legends of the Arabian Peninsula was that this Sanam had a beloved who was called Tamiya. The two of them lived as part of the Hejaz mountain chain, and because they felt uneasy about the mountains that adjoined them, they broke off from them and headed east. When they reached the region of Najd, Tamiya came to a halt. She was exhausted and couldn't go on. The pleadings of her beloved Sanam had no effect on her, and he left her angrily, continuing his journey alone. When he was far away from her, he regretted what he had done and longed to see her. So he turned back, hoping he might perhaps get a glimpse of her. But his neck had turned to stone and he halted forever in that spot. Meanwhile, Tamiya continued to burst out in tears, as she begged in vain for her beloved to return, until her tears turned into the rivulet that pours out at the foot of Mount Sanam. Some people in that region still point to the remains of the dry riverbed there as the course of Tamiya's tears.

"But is that really Mount Sanam?" Burhan asked himself, as he fixed his gaze on the dung beetles that were busy pushing balls of dung toward the mountain. He was uncertain about whether he should follow in their footsteps. While he stood for a time engrossed in thought, the insects reached the top of the mountain. Then, in the blink of an eye, they disappeared behind it. That's when he decided to climb up after them, repeating to himself: "What is there to the life of dung beetles? It seems better than the life of humans, with its idle talk and its illogic, its pointlessness and irrationality, and its endless misery." But it was an extremely difficult, Sisyphean task: every time Burhan approached the summit, his strength gave out and the pebble slipped out of his grasp, as it rolled to the bottom, paying him no heed. Then he would start all over again and push it uphill, only for his strength to give out as it rolled down the same as before. And so it went, until he found himself squeezed between a thumb and forefinger, belonging to a hand wearing rubber gloves. The hand picked him up and dropped him into a bottle that ended up, less than an hour later, on a shelf in an entomology laboratory, where he would wait his turn to be dissected at the hands of his arrogant beloved, still looking down on him.

Stone

When she wanted to tell him off so he would stop his madness and nonsense with her, and stop following her everywhere, she would shout in his face:

"How long are you going to keep doing this?!"

With a lover's firm insistence, he would reply, "Until the end of my life."

"You're going to trip over me one day," she told him.

"I'll land on you!" he replied.

"You'll be crying plenty of tears," she said. He didn't understand what she meant by that.

He continued his journey of devotion, following in her footsteps for many long years, until he was drained of energy, his back was stooped, and gray hairs covered his head. In the end, he stumbled on a stone in his path and fell into the embrace of loose earth that smelled of death. When his sunken eyes fixed their gaze on the stone he had stumbled on, he discovered it was a tombstone with her name carved on it.

Fairuz

Tariq was an expert at making comparisons. In all likelihood, he was a magician.

If he compared someone to something, that person turned into the thing he had compared them to, in a way that made them famous.

"I don't know if what they say about him is true," my father said. "But I do know a woman whose voice he heard for the first time on the radio in 1952. He compared her to a morning sparrow . . .

"And that singer Fairuz—the one they call "the Sparrow of the East"—is still warbling today!"

Mothers

The Photo

One day, Rasmiya asked her daughter to bring her the family photos. Her daughter found it strange that a blind woman like her mother would make a request like that. She couldn't guess, nor did she ask her, what she was going to do with the photos, nor did she even bring it up with her. She knew that would just make her mother angry and then she would start biting her finger until her daughter did what she had asked of her. It's a habit that some mothers have when they get angry. Her daughter just got up and started looking for those photos everywhere, until she happened to find them in a metal box hidden in a drawer. She took the box, pulled the photos out, and spread them out on the floor, in front of her blind mother, who began touching them with her bony hands that trembled like one with chronic heart problems, as though she were trying to sort through them to find what she was looking for. That's when her daughter understood what her blind mother wanted. She offered to help, but her mother firmly refused her assistance, saying, "Don't interfere. The heart knows what it's doing!"

She let her mother fumble over what she was after by herself, but what she found astonishing was that her mother started slowly picking up photos, one by one. When she picked up a photo, she brought it up to her nose and smelled it deeply. It was like she was sampling the scent of a flower, not a photo. She thought about asking her what she was doing, but at the last moment bit her tongue. She was content just to watch her, to see what she would eventually do.

Suddenly, her mother paused at one of the photos, and began sniffing it in a way that made her think her mother was about to take her final breaths.

"This is the one!" she cried out loud, like someone stumbling on something valuable. "I found it!"

It was here that her mother expanded her method of smelling it. She would place the photo on her chest for a time, while she sobbed aloud for a few moments. Then she held it close to her nose again and took a deep breath, enough to tire out her lungs, as though it were a rare aromatic plant she had at last found.

When her daughter couldn't take any more of the mystery going on before her eyes, she asked her mother what was the point of it all, especially since the photo she chose wasn't a portrait of her son who had been lost since the Iran-Iraq War, but was instead a group shot of the whole family taken in the back yard. Why was she interested in a photo like that, rather than a picture of him, just him by himself, one of many photos taken in any number of places and on different occasions: in his clothes for the Eid when he was five; on the corniche riverwalk, leaning against the trunk of a linden tree; on a football field wearing his tracksuit; on the university campus in his uniform; at basic training, wearing khaki; or in any of the other photos she showed no interest in.

Her mother was silent for a minute. She was still hugging the photo to her chest, while staring ahead with empty, indifferent eyes. Then she asked her daughter if she could remember something her brother Samir had done, more than twenty years ago, when he was eight, thinking it would make him more fashionable. Her daughter remembered.

"He asked everyone if they could wait before taking the picture, and he ran inside," she said. "He was gone for several minutes, then he came back, yelling, 'I'm ready!' I think he'd combed his hair, or maybe he changed his shirt. Ok, I don't remember!"

"It was neither," her mother replied in a tone that revealed she knew what it was. "You didn't guess right!"

"So what was it?" her daughter asked, her voice making clear that she wanted to know what it was her long-lost brother had done. "What did he do inside the house, Mama?"

"I'll tell you," her mother replied, as she sniffed the photo for the thousandth time. "He put on cologne."

Films

My mother used to think that "Maxim Gorky" was a type of tank imported from the Soviet Union, since it was uttered so often by my father, who was enamored of Russian literature and social-realist films—specifically the film *Mother*, adapted from the novel of the same name. He would whisper to me while flicking my pointy nose:

"Son, you're as fat as a novel by Fyodor Dostoevsky!"

It was three months after I was born when the National Front between the Communists and Baathists collapsed and the campaign of assassination and torture began. In any case, it was a front with a bad reputation, one that my father didn't participate in—my father, who suddenly became enamored of Indian cinema.

The Russian mother vanished from cinema and television screens, and her place was taken by the Indian mother. At the time, Amitabh Bhachchan (who my mother thought was a variety of spicy pepper) appeared with his mother in the film and the two of them sang a sad song: they made Iraqis cry useless tears. A person enters the movie theater so he can enjoy something on the screen, but two hours later, he leaves with his eyes swollen and wrung dry. But things didn't stay that way for long, because soon enough my father became addicted to watching horror movies. He skimped on our food budget for three months so he could buy a VCR to watch his favorite films: *The Shining, An American Werewolf in London, Nightmare on Elm Street, Children of the Corn*, and others.

That happened after the war broke out and my brothers were drafted into the army, just when the Indian mother, too, vanished from the big screen, once the movie theaters closed down due to Iranian artillery shelling. And so my mother replaced her—my mother, who still bursts into tears to this day.

That movie is still playing at our house.

Soot

Hamza was often the cause of his mother's ailments.

He was a troublemaker who would steal the kohl right out of someone's eye and not let a hen sit on her egg. Biting her index finger in anger until it bled, and sometimes scratching her cheeks, his mother would call down a curse on him, saying, "May God blacken your face with soot!"

At the same time, his friends, who were devoted to their families, were on the receiving end of prayers from their mothers, who added words of praise and approval for their children when they greeted them in the morning, as if each of them seemed to be saying, *May God whiten your face, son!*

They all grew up and the war broke out. All his friends were killed. They became ghosts, with faces as white and pale as death. They would haunt their mothers' dreams and drive them to longing and weeping.

Only naughty Hamza didn't die. The final bit of soot from the war continued to blacken his face. God had answered his mother's prayer as well. She forgot all about her ailments and put her arms around him, saying:

"Soot on the face is better than bones in the grave!"

The Universe

She made a habit of asking him, ever since he was little, how much he loved her.

Even when she was seventy, Halima didn't forget the question that brought her happiness as a mother:

"How much do you love me?"

And apparently, Jawad had lost the necessary means to express just how much sons love their mothers, or at least to describe it. His words and phrases became forced and artificial, and didn't give his mother what she wanted. The universe by which he measured that love was no longer expansive enough to satisfy her.

"Is there anything bigger than the universe?" he asked once. Shortly afterward, the answer came to him.

His young daughter was playing with her grandmother, who asked her the same question:

"How much do you love me, my dear?"

The girl bit her lower lip and lowered her head, absorbed in thought. She was looking for the right way to convey how much she loved her, to get the reward, a piece of chocolate her grandmother was hiding behind her back.

Finally, the girl stood on tiptoes and drew a circle in the air with her small hands, saying in the voice of someone making a scientific discovery, "This much!"

Her grandmother's delight was boundless.

Jonah

"And had he not been one of those who glorify God,

Then he would have remained in the whale's belly until the Day of Resurrection.

But we cast him out on the naked shore, when he was sickly,

And we caused a vine of gourds to grow above him."

—Sura al-Sāffāt (Q 37:143-6)

Mothers in Iraq's south are passionate about domes. As soon as they spot the dome of a mosque or shrine—whether green, white, or gold—they greet it with arms raised in supplication.

When they started blowing up domes in Iraq's north, and specifically in Mosul, I was doing an astrology reading of the ascent of the Prophet Jonah in the house of the Whale. I learned that they had pulverized his tomb in Mosul. I didn't tell my mother about it, but she heard about it on the news, and she wasn't sad about it. She never shed a single tear. "It's okay," she said. "Tomorrow we'll buy up all the gourds in the market and we'll build him a dome!"

The Ribbon

The four women in the ribbons-and-lace shop in the downtown Basra market known as "The Girls' Souq" didn't know each other. But they had all gathered there to buy ribbons for their young daughters before the start of the new school year.

The first woman bought a red ribbon, the second bought a green one, and the third bought a yellow one. Only the fourth woman bought a black ribbon. While the first three were trying out ribbons and tying them to their daughters' hair, the fourth woman took out of her bag a photo of a six-year-old girl and attached the black ribbon to the upper left corner. Then she showed the photo to the other three women, saying:

"Does that look good on her?"

Tattoo

The soldiers—Wissam's friends—could read the first two words he had tattooed on his chest before he was killed. They were I WANT. But they never learned what the last two words were, since the bullet, having entered his heart from the back, tore out a piece of his chest, and the other words were lost along with it.

They transported him to his family in the south. As soon as they opened the casket, a woman, wrapped in black and with no veil on her head, threw herself over his chest.

That was when they knew what he wanted: MY MOTHER.

Women

The Scent of Her Palm

As though he were performing a magic trick, Habib had a habit of asking his wife Hanan to gather her fingers into the palm of her hand, make a fist, and leave it like that for a while until it started to sweat. Then he would invite her to smell it, so she could guess the thing he usually brought with him, every time he came back home: a rose, an apple, a fish, a ring, a flask of perfume, and other gifts that Hanan could always figure out as soon as she sniffed her sweaty palm.

One day, Habib came home, and contrary to his usual habit, he didn't ask her to put her fingers together. She guessed that something was wrong with her husband, although he was trying to act natural and was apparently succeeding at it. She wanted to ask him about it, but he hurried to reassure her, telling her it wasn't as bad as she imagined, and that there was no cause for alarm.

"Just some minor problems at work," he told her. Then he went to bed. He didn't even ask her, as he usually did, what she had made for dinner. She wondered what was keeping him, this time, from playing his magic game with her, the game of closing her fist. She knew he played it with her every time, making her find out what he'd brought home with him through the smell of her hand. She didn't know how that happened, or where he learned it. But she enjoyed playing it quite a bit, and she had grown used to doing it.

She looked at her hand, and it occurred to her that she could do it herself. She made a fist and held it for a few minutes, until the inner part of her hand started to sweat. But when she wanted to open it to smell it, she felt there was something holding her back, something mysterious, unknown. She didn't know what it was, exactly, but she felt it was a harbinger of bad news. She felt fear coursing through her body. But what was she afraid of? She didn't know that, either. Her face, masked in sadness, knitted itself into a frown in a way that summoned up the tears that flowed copiously on her cheeks. Evening came, and then night settled in. The sun rose the next day, and she was still holding her fist tight. It didn't seem like she would open it anytime soon.

When Habib noticed all of that, he didn't ask her what the matter was. It was as if he were afraid, too, that if she opened her hand and smelled it, something would happen that he didn't want. He thought she would be in no hurry to put an end to it, unless he asked her to. It was something he never once thought of doing all week long. When he realized that something like that couldn't go on forever, he decided to put a stop to the game himself. He would ask her that evening, and nothing bad would happen. But Hanan didn't obey his request; she kept her hand shut tight. That's when he realized that she wasn't playing.

And so, she kept her fingers clenched tight against her palm, pressing tightly on them with her thumb day and night. She cooked and did her housework with one hand, until as time went on, she became accustomed to it. She regarded herself as disabled, and carried out to the end what she had started. Even when she was asleep, she would fasten her hand with tape so it wouldn't open while she was unconscious. She continued like that for many years, during which time no one ever saw a smile on her face, until one day she was found dead in her bed. Her hand was still shut tight, as if she were clutching a pebble.

Hanan died without ever smelling the scent of the other woman.

Qamarhun

Mardan had become accustomed to meeting her in the early morning. Qamarhun was a shepherdess who lived in a village beside the river, not far from the headquarters for the mechanized battalion based there.

Mardan was a driver of a Russian-made MTLB armored car, and every day, in the early hours, he would sneak off to meet her by the river bank, among the bleating of the flock of sheep and the smell of dung. But for some reason, she kept herself away from him every time he tried to approach her. She threatened to scream if he dared to touch her against her will. She told him she didn't trust soldiers: they sleep with a woman and have one foot out the door. He was forced to plead with her, while swearing to her and promising he would propose marriage to her, as soon as he was discharged from the army. But he didn't get anything in return that was worth the risk, except a stray kiss on her cheek. Anything further he could only get on the wedding night he had promised.

But Mardan, so as not to be a laughingstock among his fellow soldiers in the platoon, was determined to put on a good front while he described Qamarhun's charms to them and narrated his imagined sexual exploits with her, saying she was submissive and willing, like a doll in his hands.

"Like a talking doll?" one of the soldiers asked him. "Which end does she cry out of?"

Mardan didn't answer. He only said that they knew how dolls talk.

After his last regular leave was over, and he rejoined the barracks, he was hit with terrible news. A group of worked-up soldiers had raped Qamarhun and thrown her dead body in the river.

They had torn out her voicebox so no one could hear her cries.

The Scent of Cherry Blossom

Every day at sunset, Huriya puts on her abaya and fastens her hijab tight around her head, and then heads out to the small quay near her house. She stands there watching the setting sun slowly dwindle away in its daily circuit, and she fills her lungs with pure air. She looks around in all directions, feeling apprehensive, and when she sees that no one is around, she lets out her hair, perfumed with the scent of cherry blossom, into the quiet, gentle breeze, charged with the desires of the divers and their cries. She closes her eyes and softly bites her lower lip, as she listens to the velvety rustle of the conversation between her hair and the breeze.

Quietly, as if she were walking on tiptoes so as not to wake a sleeping gull, or a sea nymph—a *huriya*—resting her head on a smooth rock by the water's edge, or even a fish betraying its secrets to fishermen, she reaches the end of the stone jetty that juts ten meters out into the sea. She jumps nimbly onto a skiff there. Not much earlier, its owner had returned to shore, carrying in the day's catch. There are still some sea creatures clinging to his net: small fish, corals, snails, nautiluses, oysters, and colorful starfish. She picks up a small red starfish and places it in her hair, as if she were doing it in front of a mirror. She smiles at the sea, and asks the water in a whisper, "Sea, do you see how lovely I am?"

On the night of the Eid, while she was, as usual, watching and meditating on the sea with eyes of desire, she saw a fish make a splash here, and a turtle poke its head out there. She saw the lights from distant lighthouses, as the breeze plays with her brown hair and runs its soft and delicate fingers through it. Huriya heard a noise behind her and the sound of footsteps that frightened her. She held tight to the starfish adorning her hair and turned around, only to see a group of fishermen from the village swinging their oars and the axes they used to cut the heads off big fish. There was a fire that flashed like savage sea creatures in their eyes, which had widened to alarming proportions, as they demanded that she cover her hair. They drew their fingers across their throats, imitating an action whose terrifying sound she could almost hear in all its brutality: *khhhhikh*!

In the middle of this alarming display that was surging up before her eyes and heading her way, brandishing tools that could injure her, Huriya placed a second starfish in her hair. It was green this time. Then she followed it up with a yellow one and a blue one, until her hair was filled with stars. She blinked. She threw herself into the sea and never came out again.

The next morning, the morning of the Eid, the girls in the village woke up. In the hair of each girl was a colorful starfish.

The Kohl Thieves

Zahra often heard the expression that "men can steal the kohl right out of your eye." She didn't believe it, and felt it was just a fairy tale that made the rounds among women having a crisis, whose romances had ended in failure, until a day came when she experienced it herself.

That day, Zahra asked her date about it, on their first date.

"You better believe it," he told her with self-assurance.

"Really?" The answer scared her. "How do guys do that?"

"Easily," he replied with a sly smile, while taking a sip of coffee.

"And when do you do it?" she asked.

"When you're crying."

"So if we cry, then what?" she asked again.

"The kohl runs down your face, along with the tears," he said to her with a wink.

"And then what?"

"We wipe it away."

"And then?"

He rubbed his nose, and raised an eyebrow.

"Then we leave."

And then Zahra cried.

The Rose

The greenskeeper, who worked in an enclosed garden, had a habit of flirting with his wife and describing her as a rose. He would do that every day. During meals, in bed, and even in his dreams. He would call her "rose of my life," "rose of my days on earth," "rose of my soul, my heart, my dreams, etc."

One night, while she was asleep, his wife saw herself in a dream: she had become an enormous rose. Her body was densely covered in red damask rose petals. It astonished her and she was overjoyed. She expected that this metamorphosis she had undergone in her dream would gladden the heart of her husband, but it had just the opposite effect, since he wasn't acting like himself in that rose dream. He didn't even call her a rose, and it saddened her that he started calling her by another woman's name. She started to cry, so that her pillow was soaking wet when she woke up the next morning. She woke up to the sound of his voice, as he was plucking rose petals out of her body, and repeating mournfully:

"She loves me, she loves me not! She loves me, she lo—"

The Handkerchief Woman

Sawsan had long been in love with handkerchiefs, and she devoted herself to buying and collecting them. It was a habit she had clung onto since she was a little girl, when her mother bought her a pink handkerchief embroidered with white roses. At the time, she had a cold, but she never wiped her nose with it, paying no mind to the scolding she would get from her mother. Ever since that day, she was obsessed with handkerchiefs and kept buying them, until she had a large variety in different colors and shapes, and of different materials: silk, cotton, sponge cloth, *jolie dentelle* lace.

Every time Sawsan got involved with a man, she would give him a handkerchief. It was something that brought her bad luck, or at least that's what her girlfriends thought. In spite of that, she never once stopped giving handkerchiefs to the men she loved, as a kind of challenge. She was in love with handkerchiefs, and she couldn't believe that something as soft, delicate, and beautiful as a handkerchief could be the reason behind the bad luck that went hand in hand with her romantic experiences.

The first man that Sawsan loved left her after six months. He was notable for his head-spinning romantic lies, so much so that he couldn't keep himself from crying when he told her goodbye.

He pulled out the handkerchief she had given him. He wiped away his tears, before blowing his nose into it in a disgusting manner. Then he left without coming back.

The second man stayed with her for a shorter amount of time. Around three months. Most of the time he was eccentric and taciturn. So he didn't take the trouble to say those painful words, which was harder on her than a block of concrete falling on her head. Instead, he started waving the handkerchief—her gift to him—at her, until he fully disappeared from view.

The third man was by nature defeatist and paranoid. He couldn't stand to stay with her for long, and he announced his surrender by waving a white flag. That is, the white handkerchief she had given him at his most recent birthday.

The fourth man was a cheat and a crook. He played a deceitful game so he could get rid of her once he'd taken everything she had, except for the handkerchiefs. He tied the handkerchief over her eyes, and asked her to try to grab hold of him, if she could. But she couldn't hold onto anything in the end, except her disappointment and the bare walls, which she had been bumping into that whole day.

The fifth man was a sadist. But his sadism only appeared after five weeks, when he tied her hands with the handkerchief she had given to him, before he proceeded to torment her, and then he fled.

When she sensed the sixth man was about to leave, she locked the doors on him and shut him up in the house. She forgot that he was a magician, and that he could disappear in two moves: he covered his face with the handkerchief on which she had embroidered an amulet that would make him stay, and then he produced another gesture with the fingers of his other hand, while muttering mysterious words. Then he vanished forever.

The seventh man was one of those readers who are infatuated with tragic endings of films and stories, and her own life almost came to an end at his hands, when he accused her of cheating and choked her with the same handkerchief that she had given him months before, when he was telling her about the death of poor Desdemona at the hands of Othello.

There was one man left.

As for him, he killed her, and covered her face, now gone pale, with the last of the handkerchiefs she had given out.

Saltiness

Hila didn't know why the man, like the one before, dumped her after their first kiss.

At first, she thought it was because she had bad breath, or because there was something wrong with her lips. But, as the years went by, she learned that wasn't the case. She kept looking for the mysterious reason, which had unsettled her life, until at last she uncovered it.

It happened when yet another man spat and expressed his disgust at the pungent taste of her kiss.

"Where do you get all that salt from, woman!?" he asked her.

With a look in her eyes that vowed that she would never look into a man's eyes with love again, she replied, "From all the men's tears I've wiped away!"

The Night Girl

Mahar was an odd girl. She only appeared at night to sell roses to lovers on the town's riverfront walk. During the day, she turned into a butterfly that flittered through the gardens along the Shatt al-'Arab river. Since she only appeared at night, tongues had begun weaving stories around her, until finally she became known as "the Night Girl."

"Selling roses is just a front for her disgraceful profession!" said an out-of-work sailor, one of those people whose only job is slandering others while they sit in a scruffy coffeeshop along the riverbank, plucking hair out of their armpits. It was an accusation that Gharib the fisherman didn't believe, or rather he believed it, but "A friendly eye could never see such faults," as Shakespeare has Cassius say. For the fisherman loved her. He was infuriated by the men who whistled and made eyes at her as they walked by, and by the sailors who tried to sweet-talk her onto their boats. But he knew that Mahar didn't care about any of that.

One day, Gharib decided to declare his love to her. He thought that bringing her a gift would serve his purpose and have a magical effect on her. He thought about getting her some kohl, because, ever since the first time he laid eyes on her, he had never seen her wear kohl on her eyes. But he wouldn't do anything like that unless he first knew more about Mahar, such as where she disappeared to during the day, where she lived, and what her life was like. Did she live alone? Was she married? Or was she a spinster who lived with her family? He had to know everything about her, and it was inconceivable that he would marry a woman he knew nothing about.

One day, an hour before sunrise, Gharib followed Mahar and began walking behind her through back lanes, roads, and fields, and over bridges, until she passed through a cane thicket into a grove of palm trees on the opposite bank of the Shatt al-'Arab, where he lost sight of her, which baffled him.

On his way back, he was dazzled by the appearance of a swarm of butterflies in the grove. There were so many, it made him feel as if he were in a dream, and he wished Mahar were with him.

That's when an idea came to him.

He left the grove, then came hurrying back with a net, which he used to start collecting the butterflies. He collected them all. Then he committed a mass slaughter, an assault on nature for its butterflies, for no other reason than to extract the colors from their wings and collect them in a bottle that he would later give to Mahar, as kohl for her eyes.

Then he went back to wait impatiently until night fell and his beloved Mahar returned.

But she didn't come.

She will never come.

Date

What most struck Amal was the red rose that her beloved planted in her hair that evening.

The two of them were sitting in a café that was empty but for them and the waiter, who was stealing a glance from behind the counter in a way that made her doubt herself. Suddenly, her beloved asked if he could step outside to get something—a pack of cigarettes, perhaps. He said it would only take a few minutes. But more than an hour passed and he still hadn't returned. The evening went by, midnight approached, but Amal was still waiting. She pushed aside the pot of flowers sitting in front of her on the table and a soft sigh came out of her from somewhere, but she paid it no mind. She laid her head on her hands on the table, and dozed off, only to awaken after a while to a voice whispering in her ear: *He won't come*!

It was the voice of the waiter spoken up close: he was leaning back on a chair in front of her, and looking at her as if he were watching a situation that was imminently becoming Kafkaesque.

"Do you see all these flowerpots on the tables? Every one of them was a woman who was left waiting."

Amal felt scared. She put her hand on her heart as she looked nervously around her at the flowerpots, while the waiter kept talking, advising her to give up and leave.

"In spite of his cruelty and sadism, a man is capable of making lovely, sad flowerpots like the ones you see here . . . He plants a flower in a woman's hair and then leaves!"

A Face the Color of Wheat

Asad often prided himself on his brown skin, which was a different color from the other brown-skinned boys. The way he was adored by girls at school often made the other boys in the neighborhood jealous.

But Asad paid no attention to the flirtations of the girls who were taken with his charming brown face. His heart never once skipped a beat, except for Na'ima the baker woman. She was his friend's mother, who made delicious bread in a clay oven and sold it to the public. That was her profession during the war that had snatched her husband away.

She played the starring role in his dreams and in the film scenarios he pictured before he fell asleep. When he woke up in the morning, her image filled his eyes. He cried over her, for just one touch from her.

One day, Asad was going over his lessons with his friend, at the home of his mother the baker. He took advantage of her son stepping out of the room for a few minutes to confess his desire for her. She had just finished a new batch of bread when she was confronted with words of love and effusive praise. Before slapping him down with a cutting word, she picked up a brown loaf from the basket and waved it in front of him. She held it up next to his face, as though she were making a comparison between the two:

"Sorry, young man," she told him. "I've got a lot of bread here just like you: brown-faced and fresh!"

A Song

Every morning when Majid wakes up, there is a song involuntarily bubbling up in his mouth. In bed, in the bathroom, and at the breakfast table.

The psychiatrist told him it was a symptom linked to hallucination, and he suspected it was likely incipient mental illness, while a religious scholar told him it was Satan putting those idle song lyrics on his tongue, in order to take hold of him.

At that point, whatever the explanation for his condition was, Majid decided to stop singing songs this way. But he woke up the next morning singing the words of a new song. He was very annoyed. He put on his clothes, went out of the house, and started walking aimlessly, with no direction in mind, until he found himself on the city's riverwalk. There he noticed from a distance a woman sitting by herself on a bench facing the Shatt al-'Arab. He approached her, and found that she was crying. He sat down next to her and sang,

"In this great future, you can't forget your past.

So dry your tears, I say."

The woman turned to him. She wiped away her tears and smiled.

"I think I've heard those words before," she said to him. "Is it a song?"

"Yes," Majid replied. He was smiling, too.

"What's it called?" the woman asked.

"*No Woman No Cry*," he replied, staring out at the Shatt with a serious look on his face. "Bob Marley!"

Djamila Bouhired

Brigitte Bardot retired from acting in 1972, leaving behind the world of celebrity, flashbulbs, and fortune in order to dedicate her life to the protection of animal rights. Eighteen years earlier, Djamila Bouhired had left behind her passionate love for fashion design, classical dance, and horse riding, and retired from her previous life in order to join the ranks of the Algerian revolution against French colonialism. She was imprisoned, exiled, and tortured.

One night, long after that period was over, and for some strange reason, both women couldn't sleep.

Brigitte Bardot came up with the idea of counting sheep until she drifted off.

She put on her nightgown.

But she couldn't find a single countable sheep. It was as though all the world's sheep had vanished that night.

At the same time, the dead Algerians, slaughtered like sacrificial lambs, were leaping over the head of Djamila Bouhired, who counted a great number of them. But even so, she couldn't sleep either.

That night was the Eid al-Adha, the Feast of the Sacrifice.

The night of the great slaughter.

The Crow

One day, Mas'ud picked up a white crow, on the point of being mauled by the teeth and claws of stray dogs on the bank of the Shatt al-'Arab. It had been struck by a bullet, so he took it home and fed it until it recovered. It was quite rare to happen upon a crow with white feathers in that area, and Mas'ud could have sold it in the bird market in old Basra for any price he could name, but he preferred to release it instead.

But after an hour spent circling in the air nearby, the crow returned, as if it preferred to stay with Mas'ud, to repay him for his good deed. Mas'ud didn't object, inasmuch as he lived by himself in a remote hut located in a forgotten palm grove in Abu l-Khasib. He had some sense that crows were intelligent, but this crow wasn't merely intelligent: it was extremely gifted. It kept him company in his isolation and became his best friend, until he came to prefer its companionship to that of humans. He taught it some things and learned from it. He discovered that all the rumors about crows being bad luck were just fairy tales. Didn't a crow teach Cain how to bury his brother? Didn't Noah send one out to look for dry land? So how, then, could it be a source of ill-omen, and a bearer of bad news? That's what Mas'ud argued with passersby, who saw an evil omen at the sight of the white bird as it sunned itself on the roof of the hut.

As the days went by, Mas'ud discovered that, unlike those crows that are enamored of jewelry, spoons, and small knives, his crow loved to steal rags. Every time it flew off somewhere, it would come back carrying a bit of rag in its beak.

A rag stained with sticky liquid. When he smelled it, he knew it was the odor of labor pains.

A rag with dry splotches on it giving off the scent of urine.

A rag stained with dark blood, giving off the scent of menstruation.

A rag stained with light-colored blood, closer to pink, that gave off the scent of virginity.

Every time the crow brought back a new rag, Mas'ud recognized its smell.

The rag stained with vomit that gave off a whiff of pregnancy.

The rag that had spots that could barely be seen, fragrant with the smell of childbirth.

The rag that had splotches of milk, giving evidence of breastfeeding.

One rag had no stains. Mas'ud guessed it was a shroud.

It gave off the scent of death.

The Woman

It had been thirteen years since bananas had disappeared from Iraqi markets, when Jamila was given the opportunity to eat a banana for the first time in her life.

It was precisely at this point that she lost her sense of taste.

The doctors couldn't diagnose her case. They said it was temporary, and that she would soon go back to enjoying the taste of things. But that's not what happened. In fact, just the opposite: it grew worse. As time went on, Jamila lost her sense of smell. She was no longer able to distinguish between different scents—colognes, fumes, rotten smells, gasses, and different kinds of incense.

The medical profession was helpless in the face of this strange phenomenon, which began to progress, little by little, until the girl eventually lost her color.

For her, life had become tasteless, colorless, and odorless.

While she grew weak, things around her were living and growing with her. Humans, animals, and plants. Everything, everything.

She had become water.

A Woman's Heart

He was the one who first suggested it to her.

At the time, she seemed hesitant for some obscure reason. As though this was exactly the thing that would make them both miserable in the end.

"It's a game . . . Just a game!" he said to her, making light of it.

"But I . . . " she countered, feeling pained. "I'm afraid of what it will do to you, my angel!"

"Afraid of what?"

She was silent for a bit. "Of the game, of course," she said.

He kept pleading with her until she finally agreed. They agreed that they would each start repeating the other's name at a time they would both determine. And whoever got tired of it or was overcome with sleep or stopped for any reason would lose the contest, and that person had to pay the penalty: an invitation to dinner, a ticket to the movies, a stroll, a kiss, or even a rose he would place in her hair, if he lost the game.

They chose a time after midnight. They went up to the roof of the house and lay down on their mattresses, one beside the other. They laced their fingers and placed them under their heads. Then the challenge began, as they stared into the night sky where the twinkling stars were reflected in their amorous eyes.

An hour went by, and they were still absorbed in their lovers' game, which had begun to lose its fun and to wear them down. She repeated his name, and he did the same with hers. Meanwhile, it seemed to them that the more time they spent there, the more stars there were in the sky, and the brighter they glowed.

As she played, the tone of her voice grew nervous, betraying a secret fear, an old and hidden fear awakened by their game. It began to take a dangerous turn at two in the morning. She tried to understand what it was she was afraid of, but she feared she would lose her train of thought, and that would take her mind off the game: she would be thrown off her pace and lose. As for him, his voice had the tone of a confident lover, who gave no thought to the idea that he might eventually stumble, slip, and make a mistake, not realizing that a lover makes a mistake with something he knows well, which is what happened at three o'clock. At that time, they were both clearly tired, but neither of them had yet given up. His voice sounded like it was coming from the depths of exhaustion, more like the ramblings of someone suspended between waking and sleep. Meanwhile, she was making a sound like the kind in film scores that normally creates a suspenseful climax in a scene—the scene where someone happens upon the murderer, the moment when the mask comes off, and the truth is revealed. That same cursed moment when he screwed up and said—just once—the name of another woman instead of hers. That name struck her ears with a feeling more painful to her than death. The stars suddenly vanished and the sky went dark, at least in her eyes. That's when she knew what she was afraid of. It was the same fear that had come over her two years ago, when he told her about the woman he had been with before her. Instead of strengthening her trust in him, his honesty and openness lit fires of jealousy and fear in her bosom, which only the wedding night could extinguish.

To fix the hole he had made in her heart, he continued to repeat her name for the rest of his life. Meanwhile, she gave up playing and was content to watch the sky every night.

There. In the distance, in the towering heights, among the stars, she would see a sad-eyed fallen angel trying in vain to mend the terrible hole in the ozone layer.

Out for a Stroll

One day, a woman who was out with her one-year-old child saw a monkey with her young baby confined in a large cage and on display for onlookers at the zoo.

The woman and the monkey were both carrying their babies. Each of them was pointing a finger at the other and saying something to their child. They were both smiling or laughing all the while, in an obvious effort to amuse their unhappy children.

"Look, darling—like they say, *The monkey is a beautiful gazelle in his mother's eyes!*" the woman said, laughing.

"Look, my beautiful gazelle—*the human is an angel in his mother's eyes!*" said the monkey, baring her yellow teeth and giving an open-mouthed laugh.

Children

The Comoro Islands

"Blind as a bat in broad daylight is the city. Night makes it even blinder."
—Badr Shakir al-Sayyab

At the end of March, 2012, it was announced on television that the president of the Comoro Islands—the "Islands of the Moon" in Arabic—would be the first to arrive in Baghdad to participate in the Arab summit meeting. That meant, of course, that the street closures would begin sooner than planned.

The public mood turned sour, and people grew extremely irritable. People who had never badmouthed the president of the Comoro Islands started expressing their irritation with him, wondering where he had gotten the idea to come to Baghdad earlier than was customary, three whole days before the summit was to be held. To announce, just like that, the start of aggravations for people, to make it difficult for them to get around, because of the doubling-up of police patrols, the fanning out of state security, checkpoints, concrete barriers everywhere, and street closures.

Some began making jokes, saying that he came to conclude a deal with the government: oil in exchange for vanilla, cloves, coconuts, and ylang-ylang essential oil, the latter of which would be used to compete with French perfume factories. Other people considered his early arrival a good opportunity to stay home from work. But the great majority complained, and ended up impatiently waiting for the summit to end so they could go back to their jobs and normal lives.

In the middle of all this clamor, criticism, complaint, and widespread popular grumbling, only Susan felt affection for the president of the Comoro Islands and his very premature presence. In fact, she began jumping for joy the moment she heard the news. As if it were a holiday arriving the next day, and not the president of the Comoro Islands, she began repeating with childish joy—while standing on tiptoes, squeezing her hands together and clutching them to her chest, with a smile that never left her face— "The president of the Comoro Islands is coming to Baghdad! The president of the Comoro Islands is coming to Baghdad!"

She told all her friends in the neighborhood. They linked arms and twirled around in a circle in celebration of this blessed arrival. For the thousandth time, she imagined what it would be like when it happened, and the calm that would settle over the city after all the hardship and gloom. She began dreaming about those brown dots lying in the Indian Ocean, off the east coast of Africa. Each time she would tell her grandmother what she dreamed about, and her grandmother would make up an explanation that would match what she was hoping for, and which she expected would come true in the very near future.

No one in her family knew why she was so enamored of him, and they wondered, "Why is she celebrating this African public figure but not all the other presidents and kings? What does a five-year-old child know about the Comoros and its president that would make her so enthusiastic about him? When all was said and done, nobody cared much about it or took it seriously. As long as it was coming from a child, no one had any doubt that she couldn't even find the Comoros on a map.

But the night before the traffic ban went into effect, when the electricity was cut off and darkness blanketed the unhappy capital, Susan was still hoping that the president with the dark brown face from the Islands of the Moon would land his flying saucer at the airport, bringing with him enough moonlight to illuminate Baghdad's darkened streets.

The Ghost

The U.S. used a stealth fighter, a "ghost plane," in the second Gulf War, in 1991. Word got around that it could detect any light at ground level, no matter how small, including the end of a lit cigarette, which it could take as a target for its radioactive missiles. So locals would hasten to put out lanterns, "Lux" lamps, and candles, which were used quite a bit back then, whenever they heard the alert signal. It would squawk like a crow, notifying of a new air raid launched by those terrifying planes. It only made Layla, who was four years old, more scared. She wouldn't feel safe the whole time the house lights were out. She would curl up in her mother's arms, her eyes shut tight and her fingers in her ears, as she pictured the enormous ghost circling overhead, as it passed through the walls and ceilings, quietly entering through the windows to her bed to scare her.

One evening, when darkness came early, casting its heavy shadows, thanks to the gray clouds that had settled over the melancholy, ruined city, Layla asked her mother why they had to put out the lights whenever they heard the noise of the ghost plane. Her mother was at a loss for an answer she could give that would satisfy her daughter's curiosity. As the days went by, Layla continued her pestering, wanting even more to know why. She would ask everyone in her family that she came across in the house. She objected to putting out the lights while the terrifying ghost plane was still circling overhead nearby, spreading fear all over the city. But none of them had a convincing answer that would make her give up her stubborn insistence. She kept asking in a way that they found annoying.

For a girl her age, it was the kind of question that made you lose sleep, but eventually it had to be answered.

"Why? It's so the ghost doesn't see them!" her mother said at last.

But Layla wasn't persuaded by that answer. She thought her family and everyone else in the city was making a mistake, and she had to correct it.

On one of those cold, dark nights in February, when the electricity was cut off as usual, the noise of the ghost plane reached Layla's ears as it made its way across the sky, searching for targets. Instantly, as she habitually did since the war started, her mother hurried to blow out the candles she had lit at sunset. At the time, Layla was watching from her place on the sofa, in the living room, with her eyes open wide. But for the first time, she didn't ask her mother why, she didn't hide in her mother's arms and curl her small body up like a frightened cat, she didn't shut her eyes or block her ears. She did just the opposite: it seemed as though she had been waiting impatiently for this moment, in order to do something that had just occurred to her. Instead of joining the members of her family who were crowded together beneath the concrete staircase, since they believed it would protect them if the roof fell in from heavy bombing, Layla began to fumble her way to her room in the dark, until she reached it and shut the door.

The bombing intensified, and the noise of the plane, which seemed as if it were hovering around the house, filled the ears of the family, whose voices were raised in prayer and supplication underneath the staircase. Her mother looked for her missing daughter, and started screaming and calling out for her, but in vain. Meanwhile, Layla was busy in her room fixing the mistake.

After the raid, when they entered her room, they found her squatting down on her bed, in front of a candle she had placed in a clay dish. She was silent and in a world of her own, and she didn't take her eyes off the lit candle. Her father wanted to scold her for what she'd done, but her mother was wiser and more sensible: she held him off and held her in her arms, while caressing her head and asking her, "Why did you do that, sweetheart?"

Layla looked at the window to her left.

"Ghosts are afraid of light," she replied, in a voice that sounded like she'd been up all night.

The next morning, at breakfast, everyone had to pay attention to Layla as she told them what had happened the night before.

"For the first time, I saw a black ghost and it was this big," she said absent-mindedly, as she traced a circle with her hands. "I thought ghosts were white, like they are in cartoons. I told that giant, scary ghost to stay away from our house, and as soon as I lit the candle, it ran away!"

Everyone laughed, except for her father, who withdrew to a corner and started listening to the radio with interest.

"The war is over!"

The Ball Boy

Ever since he joined the Golden Shot team, Lame Hamud had
been nothing more than a miserable ball boy.

He would stand behind the goal, waiting for badly aimed shots,
so he could hop after them like a crow and bring them back to the
field. It was the most remote position the coach could assign him,
since he saw Hamud as just a klutz, rather than a player capable of throwing himself into a game. It made Hamud feel stupid;
despite his disability, he believed in his football-playing abilities
and skills, and he still hoped the day would come when he could
prove to everyone that he was no less capable than they were.
That was his wish. He wouldn't have objected if the coach put him
in for a few minutes, during which he could show a little of the
skills his teammates weren't aware of. But all year long, that didn't
happen and he didn't get an opportunity, even a slight one, to play.

Hamud kept begging the coach to give him a chance, until he
finally promised to put Hamud in the next game, which would
take place at the same time as the game his favorite player would
be playing for one of the major clubs. He was delighted and nearly
jumped for joy. He started his preparations early. He woke up in
the morning, ran out to the football field, and practiced for hours

on end. He wasn't upset when he learned that his favorite player would be playing in the El Clasico match-up at the same time, as he preferred not to skip his own team's game. He would be playing for the first time, so afterward he wouldn't have to return to his position behind the goal, where he was used to standing and waiting for stray balls.

Hamud was crazily devoted to his favorite world-class player. He followed news stories about him and collected his photos. He was fanatical about watching the games he played in, which were shown on TV. He wanted to meet him one day. But in any case, he had no hope of being a ball boy for the shots this player took, because he rarely made a kick that went wide, while the rest of his shots found their way to the goal with top-notch skill. Even so, it would be a great honor for him to get that prime opportunity, which he would certainly seize, and shake hands with his favorite player, and maybe get his autograph on the jersey for the team, which he supported.

The promised day came. I wish I could have seen Hamud as he threw himself into the first game in his life. But I did the opposite of what he did: I preferred to watch the El Clasico game that his favorite world-class player was playing in.

While I was watching that game on television, I received a painful text message on my phone, saying:

"Hamud died. The ball boy died!"

The news shocked me, and I began to wonder what had happened to this young man, and how he died. Maybe the joy he felt at getting into his crucial game was too much for him, or he took a serious hit that ended his life. Or maybe he didn't succeed in showing off his supposed skills and failed to get noticed, and when he couldn't stand the mockery of the spectators, he died of heart failure. Or he got into a fight with the players of the opposing team, and got stabbed with a knife, or they broke his skull with a rock, as often happens in games between working-class teams. I called the person who sent the text to find out. He was friend of mine: we would always spend our free time together having fun on the nearby football field. He said that Hamud was hit by a car. The poor guy: the coach had reneged on his promise to him, and didn't put him in the game, so he went back in humiliation to his position behind the goal. Before the end of the game, when his team was down by a goal, instead of tossing an out-of-bounds ball back onto the field, he ran off with it, followed by the curses, threats, and spitballs of the players. They called him lame and a loser, and pelted him with rocks. While he was crossing the street, a car hit him, and he died instantly.

Maybe he was fed up with having to take the annoying job of ball boy, and he wanted to protest, but, alas, look where his recklessness drove him to.

On TV—I don't know if it really happened or if I imagined it—Hamud's favorite player was skillfully dodging one player after another, until he was all by himself with the other team's goalie. He was now facing the goal, and kicked the ball, which went wide, flying off at an angle. It was as if he'd done it on purpose, since he stood in place, hands on his hips, and smiled at the lame boy who was running toward him, holding his ball kicked out of bounds, amid the roar of the angry crowd and their grief at his missed goal.

The Boot

In the time before there were schools specifically for deaf-mutes in Basra, Mahmud found himself in a school for non-handicapped students. He had nothing to defend himself against their hostile behavior, bullying, and endless troublemaking except his boots. He would take them off and brandish them, and with silent, confused gestures, his mute expression would repeat the insult that Iraqis use most often.

He was ten years old, and although he was mute, he was a smart boy and a first-rate student. His high marks frequently caused him problems, since they made him a target of other students' jealousy, and he fell victim to their anger. That didn't always happen: sometimes they needed him to solve hard problems for them before—and during—tests. But soon enough, once it was all over, they would go back to bullying him, and that's when he braced himself to get picked on. They would come up with elaborate tricks to play on him—putting a dead mouse in his pocket or writing an insult on a piece of paper and sticking it on his back. Or, in the simplest cases, they would force him to walk home with only one boot. He, on the other hand, rarely resisted them with all the strength he had: he either put up with it and went on his way without paying it any mind, or he confronted it, rousing himself to action by hitting one of his tormentors and spitting on another. In the end, he would just take off his boot and wave it in their faces, as a substitute for the curse word that applied to all of them.

One day, during gym, which—like art class—no one in Iraq cared much about, it occurred to the teacher that, instead of kicking the ball around in the muddy schoolyard, he should come up with something new, like testing the students on facts and improving their sports knowledge. The teacher was wearing the green uniform of Iraq's national team. He was proud of having played right fullback for the Harbor Football Club for several years, and also of having procured the autographs of both Zico and Sócrates, who were in the line-up of Brazil's Flamingo Club, when it played in Baghdad. He began by tossing out questions at the students. His first one was: "Which three national teams have won the World Cup four times?"

"Brazil!" one of the students shouted back.

"Correct."

"Germany!" said another.

"Very good."

But no one could come up with the third team. One student said it was England, and another said Spain, while a third insisted it was Argentina. The rest of them answered "China," "Mexico," "Egypt," "Holland," "Russia," "Belgium," "France," "America." Whenever a student said his answer, the teacher shook his head no—it wasn't that country, and not that one either, that won the World Cup four times. Finally a student with dark brown skin and frizzy hair sitting in the back of the classroom burst out, "Mozambique!"

That provoked a wave of laughter and mockery, which the teacher finally put a stop to. The teacher offered a reward—a football—for whoever came up with the answer he was looking for. That's when their eyes all turned to Mahmud.

"That mute kid knows lots of things," one of them whispered in his friend's ear.

Some tried to get him to give them a hint. But Mahmud, who made it clear that he knew the answer, decided to get the reward himself.

Suddenly, without thinking of the consequences of what he was doing, and even though he was perfectly capable of writing the answer on a piece of paper and showing it to the teacher, as he always did when he wanted to provide an answer, Mahmud took off his boot and began waving it in front of the teacher. He was grinning ear to ear at having gotten the right answer that had eluded more than thirty students in the class.

But instead of getting the prize and being applauded for being smart and knowledgeable, and even though his answer was absolutely correct, Mahmud that day got the most humiliating punishment in his life. Apparently, the teacher took his answer badly, and it made him roar and sputter with rage. He headed over to Mahmud to grab the boot out of his hand and beat him all over with it: on his head, on the back of his neck, on his legs and arms and behind, until that distant country was almost torn to shreds on his skinny frame. That distant country, that beautiful and happy country called . . .

. . . Italy.

Mexico '86

Although his vote didn't reach FIFA, and perhaps will never reach it, after all these years Tahsin still fervently supports Mexico's efforts to host the World Cup for the third time.

In 1986, when football fever was blazing—the Iraqi national team had just qualified for the World Cup Mexico '86, amid the flames of grinding battles between Iraq and Iran, as the two countries slaughtered each other along the border that ran between them—news arrived that the Iranians had captured Tahsin's father. Tahsin was six years old at the time.

Months passed as Tahsin looked for his father. He asked his mother about him, and demanded that she tell him where he was. One day, it happened that his unhappy mother foisted him off on his uncle, who at the time was listening on the radio to the game played between Iraq and Paraguay in Mexico.

The commentator was shouting, objecting to the referee disallowing an Iraqi goal against Paraguay. He was cursing and spitting and nearly smashing the radio, when Tahsin kicked him and asked him, with tears welling up in his eyes:

"Uncle, where's my daddy?"

"Mexico," replied his uncle, who was mad about football and

hardly paying attention to his nephew. But his distracted answer couldn't fob off the boy's stubborn insistence.

"When is he coming back?" Tahsin asked him.

Tahsin didn't get a response this time. His uncle had in fact smashed the radio. He threw it forcefully and it slammed against the wall, falling to pieces. Scattered along with it was the voice of the singer Rabia al-Basriya, as she sang like a black sparrow:

Hala hala hey!

Hala hala hey!

Ever since then, Tahsin has worn a green tracksuit and repeated the words of that song, supporting with the same intensity and enthusiasm Mexico's right to host the World Cup for the third time.

Syndrome

Kifah looked after her daughter who had Down Syndrome. At the time, her daughter Dhahab was considered—to use the former term for it—Mongoloid.

She would give her a bath and perfume her. She would play with her and caress her. She would comb her hair and braid it, and see how she looked at last from a distance. She had a sympathetic smile on her face, as she happily called out to her daughter, saying, "Where's the most beautiful girl in the world? Come here!"

Despite her condition, Dhahab still had to deal with the jealousy of her sister Sara, who was one year older than she was. It started soon after she was born, when the first indications of Down Syndrome became apparent in the little girl's looks and behavior, which differed from what they should have been for a normal girl. After that, she took up all her mother's care and attention. That didn't mean, of course, that her mother neglected Sara, but necessity demanded that the younger girl receive special care, something her older daughter couldn't understand.

At age six, prompted by blind childish jealousy, Sara angrily asked her mother, during her sister's birthday party, to which a group of her friends from school were invited—a school devoted

to special needs children, all of whom had Down Syndrome—
"Why didn't God send all of them to their original country in the
first place?"

She knew there was a place in the world, hardly ever mentioned, called Mongolia.

Dimple

One morning, Shams woke up frowning and upset because of a disturbing nightmare. As usual, the first thing she did was look at her face in the mirror. What she saw startled her.

She became sad and burst into tears, and that attracted the attention of the larks that, at that time of day, were sitting on the ledge of her window that looked out over a verdant garden. One of the larks asked her what was making her sad, and she told it, saying mournfully, "My dimples disappeared!"

Another lark that had alighted on her shoulder said, "Maybe someone stole it!"

"Really?" Shams replied in astonishment. "Who is the thief, I wonder?"

"We larks will find out," answered a third. "We'll help you recover your dimples."

The larks spent the whole day trying, without success, to recover Shams's dimples. Shams, meanwhile, was puffing out her cheeks and sticking her finger in them to leave a light indentation on her soft rosy skin, but they seemed like dimples that would quickly disappear, leaving behind a sigh that the girl let out with a feeling of pain.

Evening came, and the larks had still not come upon anything, so they returned to their nests, in hope of trying again the next day.

The following morning, when the larks returned to their search, they were surprised to see that Shams, as she looked out from the crack in the window, had recovered her dimples.

When they asked her how she had gotten her dimples back, she replied, "I didn't do anything. I just smiled."

Wordless

Huda didn't become mute until she fell in love with the neighbors' son, who was called Bibu as a kind of pet name. Ever since he was a month old, that name had stuck to him like a louse in an armpit.

He was a year older than she was. She was very shy. If there was anything harder for her than waking up early, or studying math, or the unpleasant feeling she had the first time she felt menstrual pain, it was standing in front of Bibu and confessing her love to him. So she decided she would do it without needing to speak.

She stood in front of him one day, at the time they usually spent together, in the garden at either her house or his, to review and do their homework. She put her hand on her heart, while smiling shyly. Then she pointed at him, and drew a circle in the air with her hands, in a clear motion. The point of it was to convey the idea that she loved him, and that her love for him was as big as the world.

The idea appealed to Bibu, who was stupid enough to think Huda wanted to play a game. Previously, he had seen a TV show in which three celebrities figure out the titles of movies and television serials through charades performed by a fourth teammate.

Huda did her movements again, and repeated her gestures, focusing on putting her hand on her heart. She did that calmly once, and then again impatiently. She repeated it dozens of times, but with no satisfactory result. Sometimes Bibu would think and hazard a guess, trying to come up with the titles of movies he'd seen before. A look of frustration came over Huda's face every time he said the name of the movie he thought she was thinking of: *Braveheart, Lionheart Starring Jean-Claude van Damme, Heart of Darkness, My Heart is My Guide, My Heart Pounded, A Woman's Heart, My Heart Was Refused*, etc.

At that point, she had finally had it. She wanted to fling her confession of love at his face, publicly and out loud. But she couldn't.

From then on, she never spoke again, neither to him nor to anybody else.

Huri

for Kareen Arshbawir

Two symbols that Armenians carry with them their entire life, like two crosses tattooed on their hearts, are the poet Sayat-Nova and Mount Ararat.

In Basra, when Huri turned five, she asked her mother, "Who is that?" And her mother would point to a portrait of a man with a mustache and beard wearing medieval clothes and sitting at a table beside a window that looked out over a garden. He was holding a musical instrument similar to a santour, and writing a poem, apparently, with his other hand.

"This is Sayat-Nova," her mother told her, running her freckled fingers through the hair of her yawning daughter. "Our singing Messiah and the greatest lyric poet of the Armenian people." Then she made her memorize an excerpt from his poetry before going to sleep.

The next night, Huri asked her mother, "What's the name of that mountain?"

She was pointing to a carpet that her grandmother had made for her parents, and which was hanging on the wall in front of her. The carpet showed Mount Ararat with its two whitish peaks, Greater Ararat and Little Ararat.

"That's Mount Ararat," her mother explained. "A sleeping volcano. It's where Noah's Ark came to rest and it's the homeland of his grandson, the father of our people, Hayk the Great."

Then Huri's mother said good night to her daughter and wished her pleasant dreams. But Huri soon went back to asking her questions, since she couldn't fall asleep.

"Did you say it's a sleeping volcano, Mommy?"

"Yes," her mother replied.

"But," said Huri, who was talking without making much sense, as if she was about to start crying, "what do sleeping volcanoes dream about?"

Poets

Walt Whitman's Beard

One day—it was Valentine's Day—the sky was decorated with white clouds that looked like angels' handkerchiefs. Zayd sat on a wooden bench in a public park along the river. He had just begun to distract himself by reading Walt Whitman's *Leaves of Grass* when a man sat down beside him: he was in his eighties, gray-haired, and wore an American cloth cap on his head. His beard was long and white. It seemed to Zayd that a group of butterflies were hovering near the man's beard; sometimes they landed on it or emerged out of it.

"They are shaving the parks clean!" said the old man sorrowfully.

Zayd looked attentively at him for a few moments, since he was intrigued by what the old man had said. "Are you a poet?" he asked him.

The old man with the magical beard that was sending forth butterflies thought for a bit, then narrowed his eyes and asked, "What makes you think I'm a poet?"

"The words you said!" replied Zayd. "Only a poet could say what you said!"

"Ah!" the old man sighed, scratching his head beneath his hat. "But they really are shaving the park. Look behind you."

Zayd turned to look behind him, and he saw there a number of individuals with long beards and black clothes tearing up trees from the park. He was stunned by the scene. He looked at them in anger: they were doing it to deny lovers the opportunity to share a kiss behind a tree.

"Isn't it strange? They are shaving parks and letting their beards grow long!" said Zayd in a tone of despair and frustration. The old man asked him, in a manner that was trying not to look like he was prying, if he had a girlfriend. With his head lowered, Zayd nodded yes, and said that they had a date to meet that evening in the park.

"But you have a beard, too!" Zayd added drily, while shifting away from him.

The old man smiled, nodding his head sagely and with dignified bearing. He ran his aged, trembling fingers through his beard, and out of it flew a new batch of butterflies in gorgeous colors.

"Just as your fingers aren't all alike, neither are beards, my friend," he said. He was silent for a little, then he continued in the same tone. "Take Plato, for example, Tagore, Tolstoy, Hemingway, and . . . "

"And Walt Whitman!" Zayd said, interrupting him excitedly.

The old man's chest stuck out and he looked straight ahead as if he were receiving a military salute. "And Walt Whitman!" he jokingly repeated.

The two of them became engrossed in conversation about Whitman. And while they were thus preoccupied, the old man's beard grew long, and along with it, the butterflies grew in number whenever he stuck his fingers into it. Zayd didn't notice that:

he was riveted by their discussion about his favorite poet. Night fell and they were still deep in the rhythm of conversation. Walt Whitman's beard was steadily growing and taking over the park. It spread out everywhere, like white algae. It wrapped around monuments and lampposts. It covered the swings and children's gyms, formed itself into the shape of big trees, and occupied wide spaces, releasing butterflies of all kinds, shapes, and colors. Then lovers began to make their way into the park. They had no difficulty making their way through those pure white, soft, velvety clumps. The conversation about Whitman had by then come to an end, and Zayd, slack-jawed, noticed the magical white world around him. He turned to ask the old man what was happening, but he couldn't find him. He had left the park, leaving behind his enormous beard as a sanctuary for lovers.

Wafiqa's Window

Wafiqa, who works at a bank, can't remember a single time when a man flirted with her. Even though she isn't ugly, and is fairly attractive and somewhat pretty. She puts on dark lipstick like Marilyn Monroe and puts plenty of kohl on her eyes, in a way that she hopes will entice one of those men who are attracted to kohl-lined eyes, as they are in love songs, to hear her soft, refined speech.

Wafiqa continued to transfer from one bank branch to another until, at age forty, she ended up at the Basra branch of the Central Iraqi Bank, in a fourth-floor office next to a window that looked out over the 'Ashar Corniche. Down below, on the bank of the Shatt al-'Arab, stood a statue of the poet Badr Shakir al-Sayyab.

There, through that window, Wafiqa had the first poetic dalliance in her life.

The Crocodile

After each torture session that Falah, who had been accused of a political infraction, endured at the hands of a masked torturer, he was visited by one of the jailers. Filled with compassion, the jailer brought him a plate of food and a drinking glass. He fed Falah and gave him water to drink, and with exaggerated courtesy, asked him to write a love letter to his beloved.

In return for the favor shown to him, Falah dictated to the jailer some tender words, which were at last able to win the woman over, and the jailer married her.

On their wedding night, the woman asked her husband the jailer about Falah, who had been hidden away in the darkness of an isolated jail cell for two years. Looking at her with tears in his eyes, he replied, "He died of torture."

"Why did you kill him this time?" his wife asked.

"He's a poet!" the jailer-torturer replied, in a vindictive, angry tone. "A poet, woman!"

Life Imitates Art

Suddenly, Abeer noticed the star that had fallen into her arms while she was combing her hair before bed. A beautiful twinkling star that was a cause for surprise and amazement in her. It now started to spin around her and she looked up, wanting to know where it had come from.

She assumed it was a hallucination, since things like that never actually happened. But as soon as she went back to combing her hair, another star fell out. Just to be certain, she continued combing her hair, and stars kept falling, one after another, out of her hair, until her room was filled with them.

Abeer assumed, again, that what was happening was only a dream, and that she would soon wake up out of it. Meanwhile, she sneezed, and rose petals of red, yellow, and white scattered into the air in the room. They flew up around her in an enchanting, dream-like vision. And when she rubbed her palms together, the sweet scent of jasmine wafted up. When she tucked a tuft of hair behind her ear, grass sprouted on the walls. When she snapped her fingers, a gesture in which she seemed to uncover the mystery of what was going on, dozens of butterflies poured out and began flitting above her head.

Then Abeer leaped over to her bed, and started thinking about what was happening. Like other women in moments like this, she bit her lower lip while staring wide-eyed at the ceiling. The air shook outside, there was thunder and lightning and rain. Then she pressed more forcefully on her lip and it split. A drop of blood flowed.

That was exactly the moment that the poet died.

The English Cemetery

David loved poetry and football. However, he didn't have sufficient talent to become either a notable poet or a famous football player, who might play for the English national team and score a record-setting goal.

After David finished his studies, he joined the British army, which occupied Basra in 2003, only to be abducted a year into the occupation at the hands of members of an armed militia in the city. They dragged him off to an unknown location before killing him and tossing his body in the English Cemetery in Basra. Apparently, while taking his final breaths, he had crawled on his stomach, making his final goal, right between two posts marking the graves of long-dead British soldiers, which had poems by Milton and Shakespeare engraved on them.

A Poet

At age twelve, the poet decided to commit suicide to rid himself of the despair he felt, resulting from his failed attempt at writing his first poem, which was a progressively diminishing lipogram, the kind that devours itself. He decided to devour himself too.

He started with his fingernails.

It was a habit he maintained for sixty years.

Amira, The Girl Who Loved Colors

Amira, the girl who loved colors, never put any trust in men. She refused dozens, even hundreds, of them, having no fear that she might end up an old maid.

She believed that the most important thing about love stories was their beginnings. Other than that, they were nothing more than fairy tales made up by storytellers, about people who call themselves lovers, when they were really the most selfish cheaters.

One day, a poet asked for her hand.

Since she was Amira, the girl who loved colors, she asked him what his favorite color was.

And since he was a poet, he answered with complete confidence, saying, "It's the color that a child's eyes take on the moment he is born."

But Amira held to the tradition that says the color of a newborn's eyes changes, and that it takes time to settle on their real shading. As soon as Amira heard his answer, she politely turned him down, saying, "It's hard to know for sure . . . Until he shows his true colors!"

Miscellaneous

Bull's Head

Because of his giant skull, everyone called him Bull's Head.

If anyone lost sight of this Bull's Head, they would inevitably find him in his boat bobbing on the waters of the Shatt al-'Arab, where he spent most of his time. He wasn't much acquainted with life on shore, and he only set foot on dry land when he had to, or to sleep in a hut made of reeds and palm fronds. He had built it himself on the riverbank so he could be close to the water. Sometimes on summer nights he slept on the boat in the middle of the river and the only thing that made him leave it for dry land was hunger, so he wouldn't be compelled to eat raw the fish that he'd caught. Because he was always on the river, it was thanks to him that dozens of people on the point of drowning were saved. In addition to being a skilled fisherman, he was also blessed with long experience and unparalleled ability in rescuing drowning people.

On top of all this, Hamdan—that was his real name—enjoyed an athletic physique, which he had acquired during his military service in the navy. For years, he had worked as a lifeguard during the swimming and diving tests that students at the Naval College in Basra had to take. He had maintained his physical fitness through constant swimming and diving in the Shatt al-'Arab over the years. He was mild-mannered, past forty-two, taciturn, and free of the problems that someone who lives on land has. He didn't seem bothered about being called Bull's Head, but he also loved to be called "Captain." He was tall, with a big head and, for some reason, a smooth body. He parted his limp hair down the middle, like Joachim Mahlke[1]. Basra's sun baked his skin dark brown and lustrous, like the skin of sailboat captains in Bahia[2]. He would sell the fish he caught to the vendors that came to him straight from the fish market, so they could trade his fish for fruit and dried food, and sometimes cold and flu medicine, since they knew that Bull's Head refused to accept money for his fish. Money destroys souls, he always told them.

He had a unique method of rescuing people. Although it was painful, most of the time it served its purpose. Especially if the rescuer wants to avoid drowning at the hands of the person in the water, and avoid having him cling to him in that frenzied, spastic way that illustrates the expression *grasping at straws*, and which eventually leads to the rescuer drowning along with the rescuee, thus making two victims instead of just one. Bull's Head would therefore proceed to butt the drowning person with his big, hard head, with enough force to cause him to lose consciousness, so that at last he could rescue him calmly and without interference. He would do that for pity's sake and for humanity's sake, as he

1 A character in the novel *Katz und Maus* by Günter Grass. [Published in English as *Cat and Mouse* in Ralph Manheim's translation.]

2 A coastal city in Brazil used by Jorge Amado as the setting in the novel *Mar Morto*. [Published in English as *Sea of Death* in Gregory Rabassa's translation.]

said, taking no reward or gifts. Even if someone wanted to honor him, he would forcefully refuse, saying that he hadn't done anything that deserved praise and honor, because no one dies before their time. Everything in this world happens for a particular reason, whether in life or death. Consequently, he considered himself just one of those reasons that made it possible for many people to live out their full lives.

"Basically," said Bull's Head, "it was because it wasn't their time to die yet."

Over the course of his rescuing career, Bull's Head butted a lot of heads—hundreds of them—so he could knock their owners unconscious and then complete his task properly. That method was one he invented one day, many years ago, when he was with a friend of his in the middle of the river. The wind was strong and rough. The current swept the boat away and water flooded it. It flipped over and sank. His friend, who afterward was pulled away by his life on land and who ended up dying on land, found himself clinging tightly to Hamdan, as though he were determined not to drown without taking Hamdan down to the bottom with him. He restricted his movement so much that Hamdan couldn't resist, and he thought that they would both die together. That's when the idea occurred to him to headbutt his friend and make him lose consciousness.

It worked, and from that day on, he adopted that technique as a method for rescuing other people. His head was covered in bumps and bruises, and whenever he rescued someone and brought him to safety on the riverbank, he went back to listening to the river with his two giant ears that—so it was said—were able to hear drowning people calling for help from miles away, and he would hurry to pull them out.

No one dies before their time! Bull's Head's eternal wisdom.

But, some asked, was that stormy day in June really Hamdan's time to die?

A group of fishermen who had been in the habit of quarreling with him found him dead in his boat as they passed by him. He was still sitting in the stern of the boat, with bowed head, and clutching his oars. There were seagulls circling above him. At first, they thought he was asleep, but when he didn't respond to their taunts, they had some misgivings. They came up quite close to him. One of them poked him with his oar, and he fell over on his right side into the river. His corpse sank like Quincas Berro d'Agua[3].

He died, but none of the people whose lives he saved, for good or ill, remembered him. It wasn't ingratitude, it's just that none of them could remember anything. Even those that didn't fully lose consciousness and pass out suffered permanent memory loss, thanks to headbutts as hard as steel from Hamdan, known as Bull's Head.

---

3 Protagonist of the novel *A Morte e a Morte de Quincas Berro D'agua* by Jorge Amado. [Published in English as *The Double Death of Quincas Water-Bray* in Gregory Rabassa's translation.]

Warts Like Pegs

Jabbar paid no attention to the wart that sprouted like a peg of flesh on the left side of his back, since it didn't cause him any pain or hinder his movement. He ignored it, the way many people ignore skin growths, pouches of fat, swollen glands, and internal hemorrhoids—things that stay with them for a long time, and that they may even take to the grave with them.

But not much later, Jabbar began to feel worried when he came across another wart on his right side. After an even shorter period of time, there was another one on his arm. Skin tags had begun popping up like pegs on different parts of his body, and other ones—bony ones—were growing on the heels of his feet, making it difficult for him to walk. Medical treatments, herbal concoctions, and even cauterization and laser treatment, were no longer effective in slowing the advance of those disgusting, bothersome warts, which had become so numerous that even surgical intervention wouldn't help him, since it could be dangerous or even life-threatening. He began having strange dreams about a giant peg being pounded into a big wooden cross. He shook with fear every time he passed the woodworkers' souq, seized by the delusion that just by passing by he would stir up the desire of the peg-puller tools to turn in his direction.

He tried to adapt to his shameful condition, make peace with it, and brace himself by being content and accepting of his fate: he didn't want to die because of a handful of ugly pegs. By now he had taken in stride the nickname that people in his neighborhood had given him: the hedgehog. Even when he wanted to get married, and was refused numerous times on the grounds that he would be the ruin of any girl, he didn't feel sorry for his situation. Rather, he continued to feign indifference, and tried to act as if it were just a matter of bad luck that stood in the way of his getting a wife, and not those accursed warts.

But he hadn't yet fallen into despair: he still had hopes of marrying a woman, even if she were insane or blind, and had no idea that she was married to a mass of warts. That's what finally happened one day. But misery has a long shelf life, and he brought the bride back to her family on the wedding night, while he went back to being a bachelor, nursing the injuries that his half-insane bride had given him, after she had plucked several peg-like warts out with her teeth. The next morning, the father of the rejected bride came to him, and Jabbar could hear him on the other side of the door threatening him with something terrible: "I'll give you time to think it over until this afternoon. If you don't come get her, I'll pluck your feathers for you! You got me?"

"I won't take her back. Do your worst—see if I care!" replied Jabbar, groaning in pain. "I'm not some chicken—you can't ruffle my feathers, you obnoxious . . . "

"Of course. I forgot you're not a chicken," his father-in-law replied sarcastically, and then threatened him again: "I'll be back tomorrow with a carpenter. He'll yank all your pegs out, you ugly freak!"

After that, Jabbar spent years of misery, imbibing the bitter draught of loneliness at the mercy of his peg-like warts, until a day came when he couldn't stand what was happening to him. Suddenly, he decided to undergo surgery, preferring death to staying the way he was—an object covered in bumps, like a cylinder seal, or a text copied from Sumerian tablets, filled with peg-shaped cuneiform. His friends tried to dissuade him, but he insisted on going through with the operation, otherwise he would end his life in some other way.

Then, as if it were those peg-like warts that had been keeping him tethered to life throughout his fleeting time on earth, Jabbar lost a little bit of his life every time the doctors extracted one of those pegs from him. They filled a big plastic tub with those pegs, until he was rid of them completely.

The last peg that was pulled out of his body was hammered into his coffin.

Death Stones

When Mrs. Woolf reached the river, which wasn't far from her home in Sussex, she wondered if the stones she had filled her pockets with were heavy enough to make her drown.

"Perhaps I ought to fetch some more," she told herself, while she emptied the stones out on the riverbank. Then she went off to look for the rest of her death stones nearby. She came back with her pockets filled, and was surprised to find that the stones she had previously left on the riverbank had vanished.

"Brilliant," she muttered, as she rubbed her chin and watched three ripples that had just then reached their farthest extent on the surface of the river. "Perhaps another woman got to the river before I did!"

Then she emptied all the stones she had with her, the ones she had just picked up, and went off to get more. When she got back to the river, the stones had vanished again. So she did it all over again a third, fourth, and fifth time. Her arms got tired as she returned each time and couldn't find her stones.

"My God!" she cried in confusion and anger. She put her hands on her hips and began turning around in every direction. "Someone is playing a trick on me!"

She crossed the river to the other side, after setting down a new pile of stones. She hid herself behind a tree and watched from there. And right then she saw a young girl. Another Virginia, about seven or eight years old. With her tongue between her teeth, she threw the stones one after another, skipping them in the river. The stones skipped with lightning speed, like a raptor bird hunting fish on the surface of the water, while the echo of her laughter rang out in the vast expanse of the river.

The Watchmaker

Na'ama the watchmaker buried watches that he had no hope of repairing. He would dig a small hole in his yard, then look around to the right, left, and behind him. Then he would put the watch in and scatter dirt over it as though it were a solemn funeral. No one saw him do it except his youngest grandson, who was six years old and would peek at him from somewhere. As soon as his grandfather finished burying his dead, the boy would run over to dig up the graves of those broken watches and take them out.

By the time the watchmaker had rid himself of all his broken watches and died peacefully, his grandson had grown up and become a man. He had a lot of stolen time waiting for him.

The Hat Stand

Whatever happened in the neighborhood, 'Ubayd was said to be behind it.

Disappearing water pumps and gas cylinders, broken street-lights, and fires in the farmers' market. The occupation, explosions, the financial crisis, the drop in oil prices, and the civil war.

Even when there was an outbreak of chickenpox among the neighborhood children, they said, "It's him, it's him. It's 'Ubayd and no one else."

One day, word spread about the existence of a strange, savage creature that eats the testicles of young boys. Naturally, fingers of accusation were pointed toward 'Ubayd. Everyone agreed to surround his house, arrest him, and be rid of him for good. He was late hearing about that rumor—at first, people said it was the Americans who had dropped that savage creature out of one of their war planes in order to frighten the residents—so he didn't have time to flee. He submitted to his fate and took refuge in a corner of the isolated single room that he lived in along the riverbank.

But when they barged in, they found only a large hat stand crammed into the corner. They hung up their clothes on it and began looking for someone else, someone they could hang the blame on for 'Ubayd's disappearance.

Death of the Author

Aziz the novelist was just coming to the end when he suddenly stopped. One of the characters in the novel stepped forward to announce:

"The author is dead!"

The rest of the characters heard the news, and celebrated this happy occasion by lighting a candle for the soul of Roland Barthes, except for one character who felt sad about it. Another character who was standing next to her consoled her and patted her on the shoulder, saying,

"Don't feel sad, my dear. After all, he was a religious author who was about to consign us all straight to hell!"

Foreigners

Khaldun lived in Paris for over thirty years without learning any French. When he returned to Iraq after the 2003 war, he felt embarrassed about it in front of his family, his relatives, and his friends. He invented a language in which he made exaggerated use of the *gh* sound.

Things progressed as planned. Everyone was overawed by his gibberish. Until there came a day when he was drinking tea in a café in Basra's al-'Ashar neighborhood and he heard someone talking to a group of his friends in a language in which he placed stress on the *r*'s.

It wasn't Spanish.

The Protector of Women's Dreams

Protecting women's dreams is a difficult job, but an enjoyable one. Or so I've concluded from all the long years I've spent guarding those dreams and keeping them from getting lost until they come true. They have all come true, with the exception of one dream that, like a fish that got away, slipped through my fingers and lost itself in the river.

It was an impossible dream that caused me grief and distress, since it was clear that the poor woman who was dreaming it was dreaming of *me*!

The Eraser

Every day she soaked three sets of clothes and seven pillows. She went through thousands of tissues that she tossed out the window—and which were the cause of much grumbling by the street cleaners—but not on the floor of her room, which was flooded with her tears.

Meanwhile, as she cried, Su'ad would amuse herself by drawing a portrait of a man who loved her and took care of her, who didn't cheat on her or look at any woman but her. Her wish came true, for as soon as I was finished, I fell in love with her, and I began consoling her, embracing her, and lavishing affection on her. In fact, I started crying on her behalf, while she stopped shedding tears.

To return the favor, she hastened to console me, too. Of course, the first thing she did was to promptly wipe away my tears. If only that was all she had done, but instead, she took a long time wiping my eyes and ended up erasing them, so they could never cry again.

That's how love makes us blind.

Traduttore, Traditore

Shamsuddin readily admitted that he was a failed novelist. He had written more than thirty bad novels that no one paid any attention to.

One day, a condescending critic advised him to compete for a "Worst Novel" prize. Prizes like that were usually given out in Europe. So, giving in to his frustration, Shamsuddin followed that advice. He paid a fee to one of the no-name translators that toiled in a cramped, basement-level translation office in the al-'Ashar district, to translate his most recent novel into English. He did so and Shamsuddin submitted it by mail to one of the prizes. The response, like a bolt of lightning, struck him so hard that he died instantly:

"Sorry. We don't accept masterpieces."

The Eucalyptus Tree

Riyad couldn't contain his joy when he won the bet he had with his friend, Sabah, by beating him at getting a date with Wurud. As he followed her to the market, she whispered to him:

"Go down to the river and I'll catch up with you there."

So he headed straight there. He sat on the sawed-off stump of a eucalyptus tree to rest. Darkness fell, but he didn't return home, fearing that Wurud might come and not find him waiting for her. The way he saw it, this chance he had with her was like a passing cloud: if he didn't grab hold of it, it would pass him by and he would end up the butt of Sabah's jokes. So he stayed where he was on the eucalyptus tree all through the following days, until hemorrhoids grew on him like roots. The midday sun burned him and changed the color of his skin. He would have dehydrated if it weren't for the river's flood that provided him water at just the right time. At one point, some boys crossed from the opposite bank and relieved themselves on his feet.

When spring came, the people who lived in the villages along the river began talking about the eucalyptus tree on the riverbank growing again. Woodcutters heard the news and set out with their axes to chop it down for themselves, but a group of lovers hurried to save it. They started carving their names into it, something that gave Riyad an unpleasant itch, at a time when he no longer had any way to scratch his beard. One autumn day, he felt a stubborn, unendurable pain, when a lover started carving on his beard:

SABAH ❤ WURUD 4EVER

That's when Riyad wished there was a woodcutter lying in wait nearby, to spare him from this torture.

Betrayal

Since the two of them were far apart from each other, and didn't cross paths most of the time, Gemini and Taurus came up with a new way of communicating:

Tattoos!

Each of them tattooed the shape of the other on their arm, and whenever one yearned for their beloved, they scratched the tattoo. That way, they could express their desire like a greeting, and they would feel romantic ecstasy.

One night, the moon was in Taurus, while Gemini was strolling nearby. Gemini sat on the edge of the Well of Earth to eat an apple, which she did using a knife. She saw a rope, tied to a stone, sticking out over the edge of the well.

"What is Aquarius with his bucket doing in the well that goes down to earth?" Gemini asked disapprovingly. "There is nothing but blood on that ugly planet!"

She had started cutting the apple with the knife, while repeating the words to a cosmic song about the devil tempting Adam and Eve, when she noticed the rope was moving.

"He must have gotten stuck," Gemini muttered. She grabbed hold of the rope and started pulling out her friend Aquarius.

"Don't be afraid, my dear, I'll save you from these humans. It's me pulling you up, Aquarius. Hold on, hold on!"

Aquarius's bucket was heavy.

"You must be carrying Pisces with you!" Gemini said.

Meanwhile, Taurus was scratching the tattoo on his arm, but got no response. Gemini didn't respond to his desire at that moment. His mood darkened. "She must be sleeping or preoccupied with something," he said.

Sleeping? No.

But she was, in fact, preoccupied.

Preoccupied enough to cut her hands, rather than the apple, with the knife, especially when she first laid eyes on the man that Aquarius had brought up with him.

He was the most beautiful man on the face of the earth.

[Note: This story echoes the Qur'anic account of the prophet Yusuf (Joseph in the Hebrew Bible), as related in the eponymous Sura of Yusuf. Yusuf, after having been tossed into a well by his brothers, was pulled up out of the well in a bucket by a passing caravan. In the Muslim tradition, Yusuf was famously handsome, and Zulaykha, the wife of his Egyptian master (known as "Potiphar's wife" in the Biblical account) lusts after him. She holds a banquet, to which she invites other Egyptian women. When Yusuf appears, the women are so struck by his beauty that they accidentally cut their hands with the knives they are eating with.]

A Song for Guevara

"Guevara is dead!"

That's how Ahmad Fu'ad Najm's poem went, which Shaykh Imam himself later sang. Sattar couldn't believe it, even though it was admitted by Fidel Castro himself, who had at first lied about the news of the murder of his comrade-in-arms.

Sattar continued to deny it, declaring, "Guevara didn't die!" Ten years later, when he was arrested, at the time of the collapse of the notorious National Front that had united the Communists and the Ba'athists, he was tortured: they pulled out his finger-nails and forced him to sit on an arak bottle before releasing him two year later on grounds of insanity. He was still insisting that Guevara wasn't dead, as proven by the fact that they hadn't yet found his body.

Forty-one years after Guevara's killing—in 2008, to be pre-cise—the socialist, Leninist fighter was transformed from a symbol of the struggle against capitalism, imperialism, and con-sumerism to a commercial logo. His image had migrated from walls and books to clothes and other commodities produced by clothes manufacturers in large capitalist countries. Sattar had just seen it in a television news report, on the occasion of the unveiling of a statue of Guevara in Buenos Aires on the eightieth anniversary of his birth.

It was then, just before he took his last breath, that he said, in a voice that could hardly be heard by his daughter, who was carrying out the tradition of pouring drops of water into the mouth of the newly deceased:

"This is what they wanted to do to Guevara! Guevara is dead!"

The Deadly Ecstatic Vision

Perhaps it happened during one of his ecstatic religious trances. One day, the Sufi found himself in a shabby room with a high ceiling, but no door. With him was a Japanese samurai, a lion, and a stag.

Three days went by, with the four of them living in silence and apprehension. Their hunger was clearly growing. Their bodies were wasting away, and their bones stuck out. On the evening of the fourth day, the first stirrings of the lion's predatory behavior made their appearance. With its sense of smell as keen as a dog's, the lion started probing the scent of the strong-willed samurai, and then the stag, which had submitted to its inevitable fate. But it didn't approach the Sufi, who believed in destiny and fate.

Meanwhile, the samurai pulled out a small flask and began drinking in its heady scent. The lion, on the point of collapsing from hunger, angrily asked him:

"You with the narrow eyes—what is that? Speak, or else I'll devour you in a single bite."

"The water of life!" replied the samurai. He offered the flask to the lion, who was suspicious of it, and refused his Japanese generosity. Over the course of its life in the jungle, it had grown accustomed to putting no trust in humans and their cunning. With that, the samurai drank up the contents of the flask. He smiled and said, "You, my companions in the unknown, here's to your health. Here's to this eternal life!"

No sooner did the samurai finish quaffing the water of life than the lion pounced on him.

"Excellent. You're the Yokio Mishima of your day," the lion growled as it crouched on the chest of its smiling prey. "Now we'll see how long you'll live once I've cut your throat!"

Then it roared and sank its teeth into the samurai's neck. He died instantly.

The lion was satisfied with his dinner that night. In the meantime, it put off the fate of the Sufi and the stag until the following day.

The next morning, driven by its predatory, aggressive nature, the lion moved to select its next meal. It was the stag. The Sufi still thought he was safe from being attacked by this predatory animal, since he was a vegetarian and had never eaten a piece of meat in his life. Thanks to his vegetarianism, he had already escaped beasts of prey, wild animals, and carnivorous birds in a number of harrowing adventures. That was why the lion didn't come near him or give him a single look that suggested he was part of its future plans. In fact, the lion brought the full weight of its attention down on the poor, weak, helpless stag which, in spite of its own vegetarianism, had no choice but to submit to the law of the jungle. For the relationship of lions to stags is the same as it always is, whether in the forest or in a locked, unknown room lying outside time and place.

But while the lion wanted one thing, human cunning wanted something else.

The lion approached the stag, but taking feeble steps. It tried to let out an open-mouth roar to deprive the stag of half its will to resist. But all that came out of the lion's mouth was a weak and flimsy meow. No sooner did it reach its prey than it fell to the floor in a massive heap. It kicked with its legs and let out a strangled noise, then died. It died of the strong poison that the samurai had poured out into him, although it was the water of life.

The stag was overjoyed, extolling human cunning. While doing so, it remembered its hunger, and began to smell the scent of plants.

"There must be plants nearby," said the stag. It looked at the Sufi as if the Sufi were hiding something from it. "Where is that smell coming from? Do you smell it?"

The Sufi shook his head no. The hungry stag paced around the room, saliva dripping in abundance from its mouth. It could smell the walls and the hard floor, and was looking for the source of the enticing smell.

"Plants!" it cried. "I smell plants!"

That's when it went up to the fearful Sufi, who had shrunk himself into a corner of the room. He began thinking of the technique that warriors use, that says that the best defense is a good offense. But it occurred to him that, if he attacked the stag and ate it, he would lose his lightness of spirit and his despised heavy nature would come back to him. His urine would become rancid, and his stool would stink more than it usually did. While he was in this disgraceful frame of mind, he felt the first bite of the stag's teeth on the fingers of his right hand.

Oh, what a savage animal that stag was!

The Licker

The whole thing started when he began tenderly licking a woman's stab wound.

Her wound had the taste of the knife that had been plunged into her heart by her former lover. But no sooner was she free of that wound than she turned away to another man.

Every time he licked a new woman's wound, he fell in love with her. The taste of the instruments used in the stabbings—awls, pins, hooks, straight razors, daggers, swords—would burn his tongue, until he came to know the taste of all treacherous men. If a woman wanted him to heal her injury, she asked him pleadingly, saying, "Come on, please be a good dog and lick my wound for me?"

When the final woman that he loved was cured, after he'd licked her wound, he slowly died.

It was a poisonous wound.

That is, in the end, he died of a poisonous wound.

[Note: ancient Mesopotamians believed that a dog's saliva had curative properties.]

The Exchange

Flaubert met with Tolstoy one day on the occasion of the hundredth anniversary of the latter's death. They were having a heated argument over Madame Bovary and Anna Karenina, and about which of the two was suffering more when she took the step of committing suicide. But neither could persuade the other with his arguments and evidence. At that point, they agreed to exchange these two characters with each other, in order to discover for themselves the extent of their pain.

A few minutes later, arsenic tore through the intestines of Anna Karenina, who began squirming on her death bed, dying again, while Flaubert paced back and forth across the room. Meanwhile, at that very moment, Tolstoy was in the train station looking for Madame Bovary, who took advantage of his inattention and boarded the train along with a new lover, instead of throwing herself beneath its deadly wheels.

The Creep

Isyan loved to grope women. He would go out to the market at peak hours and take advantage of the crowds to carry out what he wanted to do. He put up with a lot of whacks from women's handbags and shoes, and he received his fair share of spitting and curses. A few high heels had even left their marks on his forehead.

It was not long after the city was occupied by extremists that the markets became crowded again. Isyan pushed himself into a throng of women wearing the niqab, and started indulging in his disgraceful behavior, which eventually led to his punishment: he was arrested during a campaign undertaken by the religious morals police and was brought before the Sharia court, accused of committing acts offensive to proper behavior and contrary to Sharia: touching bottoms, looking at them, imagining the taste of them and the sound they made when they wiggled, and following the owners of those bottoms in crowded marketplaces. He stood before the bearded judge who wrapped a black turban around his head and wore Afghan clothes.

There were several criminals standing in a row and the judge was talking unintelligibly in broken Arabic that sounded like he was rubbing glass between his teeth. He issued his rulings against them one by one according to Sharia. When he got to Isyan's turn, the judge looked over the accusations before him and issued the following ruling:

"Fornication of hand of touch: Cut off hands."

"Fornication of eye of look: Gouge out eyes."

"Fornication of tongue of lick: Cut out tongue."

"Fornication of the foot of run after forbidden things: Cut off feet."

"Fornication of the ear of hear: Pull out ears."

Once all those judgments had been carried out, the court determined that there was no justification for keeping Isyan in prison, so he was released. From that day on, he crawled aimlessly on his face in the alleyways, like a blind worm crushed beneath the weight of a heavy shoe. He died after being sprayed with a deadly pesticide during a subsequent campaign carried out by the municipality.

A campaign for exterminating creepie-crawlies.

Free

In the biggest poultrification operation ever hatched in history, instead of giving birth to the male child that the ultrasound equipment had repeatedly confirmed, Hayat, like the rest of the women of the country, laid an egg. That egg would have been rapidly stamped and whisked away to the hatcheries along with thousands of other eggs, to hatch beneath the warm bellies of ostriches, were it not for the courage of its mother, who outsmarted the egg-collectors and was able to hide her egg beneath the only rooster that was in the house—just to avoid suspicion—until the egg hatched. Out of it came a male that she named Hurr, meaning "Free."

Hurr lived in the dark for more than a quarter-century. When he'd had enough and couldn't stand any more isolation, he took advantage when his mother wasn't paying attention and went out to the street one day. On his way to nowhere in particular, he read hundreds of statements and slogans attributed to the Leader. At the same time, he saw not a single picture of that mythical Leader whose name was on people's lips, invoked in song day and night, in anthems, newspapers, and poets' verses. When Hurr asked some passersby whether it might be possible to see the Leader, they answered, looking at him with suspicion:

"No one can see the Leader!"

One of them told him in a whisper that the Leader would be giving a speech to the masses that day in the plaza for public ceremonies, but he wouldn't be able to see him then either. But Hurr decided to go. In fact, as soon as the appointed time came, he hurried along with the jostling masses to see if what he'd been told about it being impossible to set eyes on the Leader was true.

Meanwhile, his mother was looking for her son Hurr, who had never returned home. She guessed that something terrible had happened to him. Ever since that day, she had searched for him everywhere, but to no avail. He had disappeared without a trace.

Several years after Hurr's disappearance, the country's dictatorship fell and the Poultry Era came to an end. The people breathed the air of freedom, and Hurr's mother set off on a new journey in search of her son, to prisons and detention camps. She discovered that everyone in the country was looking for him too, so he could describe for them what the Leader looked like, seeing as he was the only citizen that had laid eyes on him. Nevertheless, although they continued looking for him everywhere, no one happened upon him.

But recently, a photo made the rounds of the newspapers and television stations, in which an individual appeared among the crowds of people in the square where public ceremonies were held. Everyone was like an ostrich, burying their heads in the sand as the wind blew on their bare behinds, except for that one man. He was like a rooster ruffling his feathers, proud of his coxcomb high in the air, as he looked right at the Leader, who didn't appear in the picture. Apparently, the Leader was the one who had taken that photo.

A Hundred Laylas and One Wolf

In the village of Umm al-Hakawi, "the Mother of Stories," there were about a hundred Laylas. All of them, as a way of ensuring good luck, were named after the Old Grandmother—The Storyteller Extraordinaire, Beyond Compare and Known Everywhere!—Layla, daughter of Qawush the Storyteller. In the village was a shepherd called Qays. He looked just like an earwig, the insect commonly called a "testicle pincher." Qays had never pinched a testicle in his life, although no one could hear his name mentioned without nervously feeling around his crotch. He was also known as "that poor shepherd Qays," because when his rival Numayra learned about his love for his cousin Layla, he took a lamb that he owned and pushed it among Qays's lambs in the sheepfold. He did the same thing numerous times, by different means, until word got around among people that Qays was stealing Numayra's lambs, and they started calling him "the big bad wolf."

The people of the village grew angry and they appealed to the Old Grandmother for a decision. She in turn condemned Qays to death. They put him in chains and threw him into a palm tree grove next to the village so the wolves would eat him. Since Qays was an only child and had no sisters, his cousin Layla was sent to Numayra's house against her will as compensation for the lambs that Qays had supposedly stolen. Numayra married her and she bore him three Laylas all at once, while Qays, mad with love for her, had no keepsake that she could remember him by.

It wasn't long before stealing returned to the village. Only this time it wasn't a lamb that disappeared, nor was the "earwig" around to pin the blame on, so he could be driven out. Word had gotten around about a wolf nearby that was hunting every Layla that came near the river or went to harvest or had a tryst with her beloved in the thickets.

Little by little, the number of girls who had the name Layla decreased, as the wolf was now pouncing on them in their bedrooms at night, despite the intense vigilance that the men of the village maintained every evening. Tragedies were rife, and there was a hired mourner in every house. Not a single Layla remained in the village that the wolf didn't eat, with the exception of Layla the Old Grandmother. Guards surrounded her bedchamber on every side, but when they went in to her one morning, they could find no trace of her. No one knew if the wolf had eaten her, too, or if she had somehow departed without leaving anything that would offer a clue about where she went, except for a book of fairy tales that belonged to her, and which she left open. Apparently, in her reading, she had gotten as far as the story of "Layla and the Wolf."

Ever since then, as the saying goes, *"Everyone weeps for his Layla!"*

[Note: In Arabic, the story "Little Red Riding Hood" is known as "Layla and the Wolf." Additionally, this story references the Arabic romantic legend of "Majnun Layla"—the poet Qays ibn al-Mulawwah and his thwarted love for Layla, which drove him to madness. His sad story gave rise to the common proverb quoted in the final line, meaning something like "Everyone follows his own fancy."]

Soundtrack

One day, my heartbeat was stolen from me during surgery. I don't know how it happened exactly, but from that day on I couldn't feel it any more. It had been a racing beat that throbbed intensely whenever I saw a beautiful woman, but the doctor attributed that pounding to the mitral valve prolapse I was born with and which I suffered from.

I searched for my heartbeat quite a bit, but couldn't find a trace of it anywhere. My feet led me to a heart surgeon, and he told me, "You need a big dose of fear to get your heartbeat back."

So I found myself addicted to watching horror movies, although there was nothing in them that scared me, and when I went back to the cardiologist again, he asked me, "Did you get your beat back?"

"No," I replied. "You know it's impossible for anyone to recover a heartbeat he's lost, but I know where it is."

"Where?" he asked, a tone of fear in his voice.

"Have you ever heard the sound of a beating heart on horror movie soundtracks?" I asked.

"Yes," he replied, this time as though he were trying to ingratiate himself with me.

"That's *my* heartbeat!"

Then I killed him.

The Darwinist

It happened on a warm afternoon in March in the year 1950, in a village alongside the Shatt al-'Arab in Basra.

Jamila gave birth to her first and only child on a filthy, foul-smelling carpet stained with blood, urine, and viscous fluids. The amniotic sac that enveloped the baby broke suddenly and her water gushed out all at once through her vagina, in an enormous squirt that hit the midwife in the face. The midwife asked for extra money as compensation for having to put up with all that mess. Meanwhile, the child was still squeezed in the darkness of the uterus, and in danger of dying. The experienced midwife knew what she had to do in cases like that: she pulled the baby out at just the right moment, tearing it out forcefully, the way someone rips a chunk of rubber from a car tire. Afterward, she picked up a knife that was as dirty as the fish-cutting knife used by Jean-Baptiste Grenouille's mother, to cut the umbilical cord that connected him to the placenta. Then she lifted him by the soles of his feet, as though he were an animal being slaughtered, and began patting him on the back, until his blue color went away and he let out his first cry. It sounded like the croaking of a small crow accustomed to be a harbinger of bad luck and terrible news.

Six months had passed since Mansur, Jamila's husband, had disappeared. Indications of grief still lingered over his mud hut, which sat in a small village deep in the shade, more like a grove of palm trees, and divided by the small rivers that branch off from Basra's Shatt al-'Arab. There were plenty of jujube trees there, and cultivation of fruits and vegetables of various kinds. The sound of the ring doves cooing on the palm fronds outside as they announced the death of their chicks was like Jamila's wails, as she was now groaning and raving and heaping curses and abuse on the new baby.

"Take him away!" she shouted as if possessed by a devil. "Get him away from me . . . I don't want him!"

Meanwhile, Hamid, the boy's paternal uncle and Mansur's brother, was in his fishing boat, casting his net into the sluggish waters of the Shatt al-'Arab, when someone gave him the news of the birth of his nephew. So he hurried off at once and started running through the woods, taking a shortcut home. When he got there, Jamila was still groaning from her after-pains and cursing her infant child, asking them to throw him in the river. She called him a crow, believing he was the reason why her husband disappeared. Hamid came in to see her in the room with mud walls and a roof of palm-trunks and reed mats. The odor of childbirth and other fluids struck his nostrils: he almost held his nose, and then he nearly sneezed, but at the last moment it held off, provoking in him a feeling of annoyance and anger. He found his mother there: she was a stout woman of sixty, and she was holding her grandson, who was wrapped in his swaddling clothes. She was trying to quiet him down by rocking him back and forth, since he was still croaking in that same strange fashion, until his uncle spread out his hands, as if he were begging, and she handed the baby to him. Hamid took hold of him extremely gently, as though he were afraid he might crush him. That's when he noticed that he had a black birthmark on his cheek.

"We'll take him with us," he said to his aging mother, who nodded her head in agreement. Afterward, he turned to Jamila, whose groaning had diminished. She was stretched out on her bed beside the wall, and she turned her face away as soon as her husband's brother came near her, so she couldn't see the crow he was carrying.

"Just get him out of here," she said in a hopeless, weeping, menacing tone. "Otherwise, I'll kill him!"

Hamid was on the point of telling her that it was an innocent child, who was not to blame for what happened, and that it was only by chance that he should be born at a time like this. But in the end he refrained, since the hatred, despair, and ill omen the mother felt about her son seemed clear enough. The baby immediately grew quiet, as if he had found love in his uncle's embrace after searching for it from his mother, miserable about her husband's disappearance. She had threatened to kill him, and perhaps she might have, if not intentionally, then by neglect.

Hamid carried his nephew home with him. His mother, who was on the verge of tears, followed right behind him as she lamented her grandson's bad luck.

"We will keep him until she comes back to her senses," she said.

She asked her son to get the baby a wet nurse, otherwise he would die of hunger. He brought a woman who had only recently become a widow, and she was still nursing her youngest child, who was not yet eight months old. She began nursing him the same day, in return for a fee that Hamid paid out of the money he made from fishing each week. They called him Shafiq, as a temporary name, until his mother decided to take him back and name him herself. But he ended up carrying that name all his life, since his mother never reclaimed him, before she died of drowning six months after he was born.

And so, Shafiq grew and lived life in the village for eight years, under the care of his grandmother and his uncle, who moved to live in the city after the revolution of July 14, 1958. His uncle worked there for the Harbor Authority and acquired a small house not far from the Harbor Athletic Club. He lived there with his small family, his mother and his nephew. At the time, Shafiq was growing up normally and he didn't suffer from health problems. In fact, just the opposite: he often seemed active and lively, and was blessed with a superior athletic ability that eventually enabled him to become a national champion. The black birthmark on his right cheek grew as well, and soon it took on shapes that seemed like they had been picked from a basket of fruits and vegetables: at one time it seemed like a carrot, and another time like a cucumber, while a third time like a corncob, until he was twelve and it came to look like a banana that had been left too long in the fridge and turned black. Because of that, there was a strange animal-like fur growing on his birthmark, which Shafiq continued to feel bothered and embarrassed about, until one day he nearly tore it off by scratching it so hard. But once the birthmark stopped growing and getting wider, he began to make peace with its shape and the fact that it was on his face like a patch of skin someone had forcibly stuck on him to compensate for the dimple on his chin.

Mansur, Shafiq's father, spent the final years of his life believing in the theory of evolution that Marx embraced when Engels came to him carrying a newspaper that had published it. Later it became the foundation from which he set out to prove his social theory and his other theory on economics. Mansur was one of those educated leftists that the Communist Party's Central Committee dispatched to take advantage of their presence as teachers in remote schools, to educate villagers and peasants and win them over under the slogan "Workers and Peasants of Arab Lands, Unite!", which the former Iraqi Communist Party secretary "Comrade Fahd" had written himself, and to instruct them in the goals of the global proletariat—"Eight hours of work, eight hours of rest, eight hours of culture"—in a shack overlooking the river. Mansur was daring to the point of recklessness as he publicly declared that man descended from monkeys. He said that in front of his pious opponents in the village, who adhered to the Qur'anic concept that people could be changed into animals as punishment. They themselves hoped the day would come when Mansur would turn into a monkey, something that Shaykh Habibullah, the imam of the village mosque, assured them would happen sooner or later, every time he ascended the pulpit just after the Friday prayer, as he angrily repeated in a threatening tone:

"That Darwinist infidel—one day he'll be turned into a monkey, so he can see for himself!"

But the sermons and intimidation of Shaykh Habibullah had no effect on Mansur, nor did the threats of murder that he received from extremists change his conviction about this. Ever since he read Darwin's book, *The Origin of Species*, he spread the word everywhere he went about the theory that humans descended from monkeys. He would stir up anger, even from his wife, who threatened to leave him if he didn't stop pushing that idea. But she soon returned to his arms, heedless of what his reputation had become because he embraced that theory: people mocked him and considered him an unbeliever. She loved him, and her life with him was a love story that women in the village still talk about.

She would joke with him in bed, saying, "I would love you even if you were a monkey!"

"You're the most beautiful monkey in the world," he would reply.

She was three months pregnant when she felt a pregnancy craving. She craved a banana, at a time when that fruit—which was grown in Basra back then—wasn't yet in season. Despite that, Mansur decided to risk sneaking into an orchard belonging to a large landowner, hoping to happen upon at least a single banana on one of the few banana trees there. But he first had to make his way across a number of jujube orchards to get to where he wanted to go.

Jamila wasn't reassured, and regretted having told him about her banana cravings, especially since she knew how stubborn her husband was, and how he wouldn't back down once he'd decided on something, even if his decisions were in response to desires that he didn't believe would lead to great consequences if they weren't fulfilled, like a woman's fear that her child would come into the world with a shameful birthmark in the shape of the thing she wanted to eat. A feeling of worry, fear, and grief began to overpower her from the first moment her husband left the house in search of a banana. As if she knew he would never come back, Jamila cried before he left, while pressing her hands to her cheeks and focusing her eyes on his. In fact, Mansur didn't come back that night, nor the next day, nor the days that followed. He vanished in one of the jujube orchards spread out along the right-hand bank of the Shatt al-'Arab, where cargo ships laden with goods pass by on their way to the Maqal port facility. He didn't return home, nor did anyone see him come out of the orchard. Some people claimed to know somehow that he had drowned, and they thought it more likely that he had died that way than from a snake bite, or a scorpion, or from one of those evil things that come up from under the earth and snatch men away. But none of them took the trouble to look for him, seeing as how he had traced their origins to animals and said they were monkeys. The only exception was his family and some of his relatives, who began looking in the rivers, dense orchards, and nearby villages, hoping that perhaps they would stumble upon a trace of him, before they lost all hope and informed the police that he had gone missing. At that point, when the police also couldn't find any piece of evidence that would lead them to find out what happened to him, all that was left was the likelihood that he had drowned in the Shatt al-'Arab, even though everyone testified that he was a skilled swimmer. In those regions, there were two special skills that all the male inhabitants of the villages along the Shatt are necessarily good at: swimming and climbing palm trees. Mansur was no less skilled in the latter than in the former. There are other factors that might help explain the drowning deaths of those who are good at swimming, the most common being when someone is struck with a muscle cramp in one of their legs, preventing them from being able to move while swimming in deep water. Similarly, it might have been the case that a sea snake or a giant turtle or a hungry shark in the Gulf that had slipped into the mouth of the Shatt in search of cooler waters, took a bite out of the swimmer's foot and caused him to drown. But in the meantime, nothing turned up to indicate that Mansur had met his death that way. As for the possibility that his disappearance was due to a female jinn that inhabited the Shatt or to a mermaid, they were fairy tales like those told only by aged grandmothers who weave stories to frighten young children on cold nights.

Jamila couldn't deal with the shock of her husband's disappearance.

According to her, his disappearance was more oppressive and painful than death, despite the hope that people leave behind them that they will be found again one day. She always pictured the dark side of things, the blackish side, the worst part of which was its process of transformation that turned the hope of finding the disappeared person into the hope of stumbling upon his corpse. And when there is no corpse, then the search for a name begins—just finding their name on a register of missing people. And when you can't find a name, then you bite your nails with regret and distress over a life spent waiting for a phantom, a Godot that isn't there, nothing, mere dust. So Jamila made up her mind to get rid of the child, as if she were doing it to cure herself of her bitterness and punish him for his father's disappearance. She harbored feelings of hatred for him, considering him bad luck and an evil omen that gave her no hope of her husband ever coming back.

One day, Jamila threw herself from a height, almost breaking her leg. Another day, she swallowed a lot of pills, then drank liquids that inflamed her stomach and made her nauseous for a long while. She did everything in her power to abort him, but she couldn't; it was as if he were tied to her insides with ropes. She felt it was hopeless and after two months she stopped trying. She decided to have the baby, so that afterward she could throw him in the river, or in a well, or in front of the mosque. If she was forced to, she would toss him in the nearest dumpster as food for stray dogs. She would have done that eventually, but his uncle Hamid was there that day, and he rescued him at just the right time.

Three days after he was born, that is, six months after his father's disappearance, during the annual harvest season, the farmers began to notice a decrease in the jujube yield. As time went by, a lot of trees were damaged: their branches were broken and they had been violently shaken so that their fruits had been shaken off. Tons of jujubes covered the ground, smashed and left to dry and rot or be eaten by worms. The farmers were furious. They had no doubt that someone was doing it on purpose, to put them in a position where they would have no way of defending themselves from suspicions of sabotage and carelessness that the large landowners would pin on them. At first, they suspected the Communist cell that Mansur had formed and which met in secret in one of the demolished orchards, especially since they were aware of the Communists' hatred for big landowners. Some of the strange terminology they were using reached their ears, such as "bourgeoisie," "proletariat," "socialism," "capitalism," and "Darwinism." But they then retracted the accusation against the Communists, since some of the farmers had sons that belonged to that cell, and thus they wouldn't set out to harm their farmworker fathers, since they were well aware of the punishments that would fall on their families as a consequence.

In the end, the farmworkers settled the matter by resolving to discover who was doing it, catch him, and stop him from causing them any more harm. They began walking through the orchards by day with their staffs and sickles, and at night they would select a group to keep watch, until one moonlit night, they fell upon the culprit that had made them lose sleep all that time. They discovered that there was a monkey behind all that nonsense.

A big, strong, ill-tempered monkey. They saw it leap from one tree to another and hang by its branches, as it attacked them with seeds of the jujubes it was stealing every day. Seeing that turned some of those who opposed the theory of evolution and who expected a terrible fate for Mansur, especially Shaykh Habibullah, into believers in the Qur'anic theory of human metamorphosis into animals. The shaykh climbed the steps of the pulpit—it was a Friday—and in a tone of intense satisfaction and Schadenfreude, made public the news that Mansur the Darwinist, the communist, the unbeliever, had been turned into a monkey. He spared no effort after that to whip up enthusiasm for killing that mad, trouble-making monkey. Some of his extremist followers would have taken care of that, but Mansur's tribe stood in their way. They proposed arresting him and just putting him in jail. But none of the farmworkers' attempts to catch him were successful. That damned monkey was just too skilled at the arts of deceit, concealment, cunning, and firing jujube seeds at them. It was like he was shooting them out of a rifle, rather than out of his mouth. As time went on, his activity increased, making life miserable for the farmworkers and causing greater losses for the landowners. After he had stripped the jujube trees of their fruit, he moved on to the palm trees and began ripping out their floral-stem spadixes. In a matter of days, there was not a single flowering seed left in the palm trees. The ground was covered with white spadix pollen. At that point, Shaykh Habibullah decided to murder him in secret, with a rifle he'd acquired thirty-six years previously from a Turkish conscript who was fleeing from the Ottoman army's battles with the English, in exchange for Habibullah offering him shelter. He assigned this task to one of his followers who was good at hunting.

But then something happened that Shaykh Habibullah hadn't taken account of. On the same day he decided to murder the monkey, everyone was surprised by two Indian ship's officers who were searching the area for a monkey that had escaped from the ship they worked on, while it was moored on the shoreline that faced the village. They had a female monkey named Lucy with them. They said she was the monkey's mate, and they brought her along with them in the hope of persuading him to come back to the ship. Shaykh Habibullah was furious. He would have turned them away and gone ahead with his murder plan, but some farmworkers got there ahead of him and let the officers know where the monkey was. The two officers made their way into the orchards to look for it, accompanied by Lucy the monkey, who was carrying with her some bananas for her husband. The villagers' ears had become deaf with all her noise, until it seemed as if she were a woman longing to see her husband after a long absence. Some women hurried to Jamila and whispered in her ear about what was going on there. As if Lucy had truly hurt her, the woman fumed with rage, tearing at her clothes and slapping her cheeks. Then she got up and started running barefoot toward the orchards, screaming and wailing all the way. By then, Lucy had fully completed her mission: she was able to lure the escaped monkey to her, and the two Indians grabbed him, tied him up, and put him on a rowboat back to the ship, so they could then finish taking him to Medina, where a rich man had decided to build a zoo.

On the other hand, those who supported the animal-metamorphosis hypothesis had suffered a reversal and had scowls on their faces, just when they had been on the point of believing that Mansur had in fact turned into a monkey. There was no trace of him anywhere. Maybe he really had drowned, or he'd been knocked off by the big landowners, or by the extremists who had already threatened him, or maybe he'd been torn apart by a wild animal—a hypothesis that was refuted by the lack of bones or the remains of his corpse.

Days passed, and people would have almost forgotten about him, if one of the farmworkers hadn't started the fuss about him again during the next harvest season, when he claimed to have suffered from an attack of jujube seeds in an orchard.

Meanwhile, Shafiq was now two weeks old, and had now lost both his parents: his mother had drowned in the waters of the Shatt al-'Arab when she tried to catch up to the rowboat bringing the monkey and his wife Lucy to the ship. And so, it fell to Hamid to care for his nephew on a permanent basis, after the rest of Mansur's family declined the responsibility of raising him, a responsibility he couldn't abandon. From that point on, Shafiq enjoyed the care and protection of his bachelor uncle and his paternal grandmother. It wasn't hard for them to provide a decent life for a small, orphaned child. They surrounded him with everything he needed in the way of support, and lavished him with love, showing him affection all the time as they tried to shield him from the memory of the painful past, something others didn't want to forget. Shafiq was hardly four years old when children in the street began calling him the monkey's son. It didn't stop there, but grew to become dangerous for him some years later, when a group of boys ganged up to bully him. They would constantly pick on him from the moment he entered school. He ended up suffering the consequences of his father's belief in Darwinism. Even though the story about his father's metamorphosis into a monkey had been disproven—after it had become clear that the monkey who wrecked the jujube orchards wasn't the missing Mansur—there were those who still called Shafiq a monkey, and sometimes the son of a monkey. That was what drove Uncle Hamid to leave for the city, to keep him away from the bitterness of life in a village where most of the inhabitants still believed that his father had been turned into a monkey.

In the life of the city, little Shafiq found a space and a fresh start to realize his athletic dreams, which took shape early in life, as he took advantage of living in a neighborhood that had one of Iraq's most established athletic clubs. He started with football when he was ten, after which he moved on to running, and from there to basketball, before arriving eventually at wrestling. He was on the national wrestling team for over ten years, during which time he won lots of medals and titles. He finished his schooling and graduated from the College of Physical Education. After that, during his military service, he joined the army's athletic games. Then he was called up again to do reserve service for the army when the Iran-Iraq War broke out. When the war ended in 1988, Shafiq was thirty-eight years old, a married father of three sons, and was living in the same house that his uncle Hamid had left for him: Hamid had gone back to the village after he retired and his mother died, to live out his final days there.

After the war, Shafiq went back to sports, and briefly worked as a coach for a wrestling team in the city, before an opportunity presented itself to him to work in the local radio station, first as a sports commentator, then as a presenter for the morning physical fitness program. It was the last job he held before he was lost in the regime's prisons.

Up to that point, he had possessed a trim body and a lively mind. He was active, full of life and devoted to it. He loved to joke around and woke up with the first crowing of the rooster that he had acquired specifically to wake him up in those early hours, so he could begin his morning exercise routine of running, weightlifting, and acrobatics. He would shave, shower, and have his breakfast—a raw egg, a slice of brown bread, and a cup of fresh water-buffalo milk which he bought from the women who sold cheese in the market. He would put on his tracksuit and go on foot to the radio station to record a new episode of his weekly program, which was about getting into shape and building healthy bodies, by presenting advice to his listeners about healthy eating, and by explaining appropriate ways to shed excess weight. He would devote half of each episode to talking about the health benefits of foods—a certain fruit or a type of vegetable or nuts. He didn't stop there: in fact, he would bring a bag full of that kind of food with him and start handing it out among his station colleagues, as he related over the microphone some anecdotes about food; they were quirky and sometimes sarcastic. After explaining to his listeners the benefits of carrots, for example, he might segue into talking about rabbits, or tell amusing stories about walnuts and their connection with squirrels, or bears' relationship with honey.

One day, his wife felt a craving for bananas. She was pregnant with her fourth child.

Shafiq scratched the birthmark on his cheek as a kind of involuntary response as soon as he heard his wife complain about feeling nauseous while asking for bananas. It had been so long since he had put his hand on his birthmark that he sometimes forgot that there was a birthmark on his face that looked like a banana. But once he heard his wife beseech him to bring her bananas, he started scratching his cheek, as though he'd been struck by an itch. In his thirty-eight years of living, he hadn't eaten so much as a peel from a banana. They had been hard to find in the markets since the beginning of the eighties, for obscure reasons known only to the government. He thought about ignoring his wife's pregnancy cravings, but she had become so insistent that he thought to himself she would die if she didn't eat some bananas. He remembered that a birthmark had appeared on his cheek because his mother didn't get to eat bananas, so he gave up his idea and decided to go out to look for bananas after all. While he was on his way to the market, he thought it would be a good idea to devote the next episode of his program to bananas, and he would explain their health benefits and importance. He decided to buy an extra kilo, so he could hand them out to his colleagues at the station, as he was accustomed to doing every time. But he couldn't find the slightest trace of a banana in the market. He looked everywhere, and started going from market to market, and asked the vendors, but to no avail.

"My God, Basra couldn't possibly be out of bananas!" he thought angrily.

He thought about his child about to be born, and how he would come into this world with a birthmark in the shape of a banana stuck to his cheek, or his forehead, or maybe his neck. He pictured him surrounded by a group of rude boys asking him the same question he was asked when he was little, about whether that birthmark was really a banana, or a penis that his mother lusted after when he was a fetus in her stomach. He couldn't stand the scene he was imagining, and he went back the house carrying a bag filled with oranges, but his wife refused to eat anything except bananas. She instantly burst into tears, putting on a show of wanting to be pampered:

"I want bananas!"

She was fiddling with the zipper of the jacket of his tracksuit, pouting, and shrugging her shoulders, the way children do:

"I really want some bananas now!"

Meanwhile, he was thinking about the new episode of his program.

The next day, Shafiq went to the station, and on his way there he noticed a long convoy of military trucks carrying tanks. It seemed as if it stretched all the way to the Soviet Union. His face turned pale while he counted those tanks and wondered how much just one of them would cost. They were passing in front of him on their way to the Kuwaiti border, only to be destroyed two years later when American planes turned them into scrap metal. He grew greatly worried. The smile vanished from his face, to be replaced by a look of annoyance. It caught the attention of his colleagues, who noticed that this time he came with his hands empty—no walnuts, no carrots, no honey, not even bananas. They found it strange when he asked them about the cost of a tank that the government was importing from the Soviet Union.

"I think it's four million dollars," one of his colleagues replied.

Shafiq was startled, as the number alarmed him. He began counting on his fingers and would have declared it an act of stupidity, if one of his colleagues hadn't winked at him at that moment, to indicate the presence of an employee there who spied for the government. Afterward, he entered the studio and sat in his seat in front of the microphone. The director pointed to him that they were starting, and he began by greeting his listeners with an indifference that was unusual for him, beginning his talk about the benefits of bananas:

"Every citizen should eat at least one banana a day!"

Then he began, as usual, telling jokes related to the topic of that day's episode:

"Friends, did you know that bananas used to be grown in Basra? That monkeys love bananas, and eat them more than we do? Speaking of monkeys, Descartes says that they used to be able to speak, but they went silent so that they wouldn't be forced to work—ha ha! Picture with me, if you will, a monkey talking to a farmer on one of the islands off Ecuador, asking him in a pleading tone: 'Please good farmer, won't you give me a banana? My pregnant wife is craving a banana, and if she doesn't eat it, a birthmark will grow on my child's rear end, and you know how much of a blemish that will be. Right, nice farmer? Pull one off the tree and toss it to me, yes, let me have it, like that, now!' Speaking of which, there is a little story I heard from my grandmother when I was little, when I asked her why bananas are curved. She said that bananas come out straight, like carrots and cucumbers, but there are monkeys that bend them in the harbor, and they come to us looking like that—curved!"

He grew more sarcastic during the final minute of the program, which he concluded with a discussion that was the noose he tied around his own neck:

"More than a hundred billion bananas are eaten worldwide every year. Monkeys are responsible for only a third of that! And our government buys one tank from the Soviet Union for four million dollars! At a time when our markets have no bananas!"

Shafiq didn't return home that day: less than an hour after his program ended, a force from the government's security services arrested him. They tied him up, blindfolded him, and brought him in a car with tinted windows to the headquarters of the intelligence services. They stripped him of his clothes and put him in an isolated cell, and prevented his wife from visiting him. They denied him food until he almost died of hunger. Then they began to gradually feed him.

His food in the first week consisted of a banana and a cup of water. The second week, it was two bananas and a half cup of water, and the third week it was three bananas and a quarter-cup of water. Starting from the fourth week, his food in prison was limited to just bananas, with one cup of water a day. There were a lot of bananas: he wished he could send just one of them to his wife, so he could avoid the possibility that his child would be born with a banana-shaped birthmark on his cheek. The first symptoms of illness had begun to show on the first week, when he began suffering from insomnia and intense diarrhea, followed by a migraine headache and neurological damage. His teeth rotted and he had a dangerous weight growth, before he was struck by diabetes and was close to death.

While he was dying in his solitary cell, expecting at any moment to take his final breath, the birthmark began to expand, but slowly. At first, it covered the right side of his face, where it was located, then it moved to the other side, before covering his face completely and creeping over his head. The more the birthmark expanded, flowing out completely over his skin, the more his skin changed. It became rougher, with a long dark-colored fur that spread out all over his body, with the exception of his behind and his face, which were on the pink side. His features changed remarkably. His body shrank in a terrifying way. His hands grew long and his feet grew short. The two big toes on both his feet came to look a lot like thumbs, which made it possible for him to grab things with his feet. His nails flattened out. He forgot how to speak and began letting out noises like a guffaw. His nose stuck out in front, he came to have thin lips, a wide jaw, long incisors, a small nose, deep-set eyes, and two big round ears, while there was a small protrusion above his behind that continued to grow and eventually turned into a tail.

The torturers observed these stages of evolution with astonishment. They were terrified by the gradual transformation of the man into an enormous birthmark in the shape of a chimpanzee that stained the face of humanity.

PARTNERS

pixel ||| texel

EMBREY FAMILY
FOUNDATION

ADDITIONAL DONORS, CONT'D

Mark Haber
Mary Cline
Maynard Thomson
Michael Reklis
Mike Soto
Mokhtar Ramadan
Nikki & Dennis Gibson
Patrick Kukucka
Patrick Kutcher
Rev. Elizabeth & Neil Moseley
Richard Meyer

Scott & Katy Nimmons
Sherry Perry
Sydneyann Binion
Stephen Harding
Stephen Williamson
Susan Carp
Susan Ernst
Theater Jones
Tim Perttula
Tony Thomson

SUBSCRIBERS

Margaret Terwey
Ben Fountain
Gina Rios
Elena Rush
Courtney Sheedy
Caroline West
Brian Bell
Charles Dee Mitchell
Cullen Schaar
Harvey Hix
Jeff Lierly
Elizabeth Simpson

Nicole Yurcaba
Jennifer Owen
Melanie Nicholls
Alan Glazer
Michael Doss
Matt Bucher
Katarzyna Bartoszynska
Michael Binkley
Erin Kubatzky
Martin Piñol
Michael Lighty
Joseph Rebella

Jarratt Willis
Heustis Whiteside
Samuel Herrera
Heidi McElrath
Jeffrey Parker
Carolyn Surbaugh
Stephen Fuller
Kari Mah
Matt Ammon
Elif Ağanoğlu

AVAILABLE NOW FROM DEEP VELLUM

SHANE ANDERSON · *After the Oracle* · USA

MICHÈLE AUDIN · *One Hundred Twenty-One Days* · translated by Christiana Hills · FRANCE

BAE SUAH · *Recitation* · translated by Deborah Smith · SOUTH KOREA

MARIO BELLATIN · *Mrs. Murakami's Garden* · translated by Heather Cleary · *Beauty Salon* · translated by Shook · MEXICO

EDUARDO BERTI · *The Imagined Land* · translated by Charlotte Coombe · ARGENTINA

CARMEN BOULLOSA · *Texas: The Great Theft* · *Before* · *Heavens on Earth* · translated by Samantha Schnee · Peter Bush · Shelby Vincent · MEXICO

MAGDA CARNECI · *FEM* · translated by Sean Cotter · ROMANIA

LEILA S. CHUDORI · *Home* · translated by John H. McGlynn · INDONESIA

MATHILDE CLARK · *Lone Star* · translated by Martin Aitken · DENMARK

SARAH CLEAVE, ed. · *Banthology: Stories from Banned Nations* · IRAN, IRAQ, LIBYA, SOMALIA, SUDAN, SYRIA & YEMEN

LOGEN CURE · *Welcome to Midland: Poems* · USA

ANANDA DEVI · *Eve Out of Her Ruins* · translated by Jeffrey Zuckerman · MAURITIUS

PETER DIMOCK · *Daybook from Sheep Meadow* · USA

CLAUDIA ULLOA DONOSO · *Little Bird,* translated by Lily Meyer · PERU/NORWAY

RADNA FABIAS · *Habitus* · translated by David Colmer · CURAÇAO/NETHERLANDS

ROSS FARRAR · *Ross Sings Cheree & the Animated Dark: Poems* · USA

ALISA GANIEVA · *Bride and Groom* · *The Mountain and the Wall* · translated by Carol Apollonio · RUSSIA

FERNANDA GARCIA LAU · *Out of the Cage* · translated by Will Vanderhyden · ARGENTINA

ANNE GARRÉTA · *Sphinx* · *Not One Day* · *In/concrete* · translated by Emma Ramadan · FRANCE

JÓN GNARR · *The Indian* · *The Pirate* · *The Outlaw* · translated by Lytton Smith · ICELAND

GOETHE · *The Golden Goblet: Selected Poems* · *Faust, Part One* · translated by Zsuzsanna Ozsváth and Frederick Turner · GERMANY

SARA GOUDARZI · *The Almond in the Apricot* · USA

NOEMI JAFFE · *What Are the Blind Men Dreaming?* · translated by Julia Sanches & Ellen Elias-Bursac · BRAZIL

CLAUDIA SALAZAR JIMÉNEZ · *Blood of the Dawn* · translated by Elizabeth Bryer · PERU

PERGENTINO JOSÉ · *Red Ants* · MEXICO

TAISIA KITAISKAIA · *The Nightgown & Other Poems* · USA

SONG LIN · *The Gleaner Song: Selected Poems* · translated by Dong Li · CHINA

JUNG YOUNG MOON · *Seven Samurai Swept Away in a River* · *Vaseline Buddha* · translated by Yewon Jung · SOUTH KOREA

KIM YIDEUM · *Blood Sisters* · translated by Ji yoon Lee · SOUTH KOREA

JOSEFINE KLOUGART · *Of Darkness* · translated by Martin Aitken · DENMARK

YANICK LAHENS · *Moonbath* · translated by Emily Gogolak · HAITI

FOUAD LAROUI · *The Curious Case of Dassoukine's Trousers* · translated by Emma Ramadan · MOROCCO

FORTHCOMING FROM DEEP VELLUM

MARIO BELLATIN • *Etchapare* • translated by Shook • MEXICO

CAYLIN CARPA-THOMAS • *Iguana Iguana* • USA

MIRCEA CĂRTĂRESCU • *Solenoid* • translated by Sean Cotter • ROMANIA

TIM COURSEY • *Driving Lessons* • USA

ANANDA DEVI • *When the Night Agrees to Speak to Me* • translated by Kazim Ali •
MAURITIUS

DHUMKETU • *The Shehnai Virtuoso* • translated by Jenny Bhatt • INDIA

LEYLÂ ERBIL • *A Strange Woman* •
translated by Nermin Menemencioğlu & Amy Marie Spangler • TURKEY

ALLA GORBUNOVA • *It's the End of the World, My Love* •
translated by Elina Alter • RUSSIA

NIVEN GOVINDEN • *Diary of a Film* • GREAT BRITAIN

GYULA JENEI • *Always Different* • translated by Diana Senechal · HUNGARY

DIA JUBAILI • *No Windmills in Basra* • translated by Chip Rosetti • IRAQ

ELENI KEFALA • *Time Stitches* • translated by Peter Constantine • CYPRUS

UZMA ASLAM KHAN • *The Miraculous True History of Nomi Ali* • PAKISTAN

ANDREY KURKOV • *Grey Bees* • translated by Boris Dralyuk • UKRAINE

JORGE ENRIQUE LAGE • *Freeway La Movie* • translated by Lourdes Molina • CUBA

TEDI LÓPEZ MILLS • *The Book of Explanations* • translated by Robin Myers • MEXICO

ANTONIO MORESCO • *Clandestinity* • translated by Richard Dixon • ITALY

FISTON MWANZA MUJILA • *The Villain's Dance* • translated by Roland Glasser •
DEMOCRATIC REPUBLIC OF CONGO

N. PRABHAKARAN • *Diary of a Malayali Madman* •
translated by Jayasree Kalathil • INDIA

THOMAS ROSS • *Miss Abracadabra* • USA

IGNACIO RUIZ-PÉREZ • *Isles of Firm Ground* • translated by Mike Soto • MEXICO

LUDMILLA PETRUSHEVSKAYA • *Kidnapped: A Crime Story* •
translated by Marian Schwartz • RUSSIA

NOAH SIMBLIST, ed. • *Tania Bruguera: The Francis Effect* • CUBA

S. YARBERRY • *A Boy in the City* • USA